Isabelle

BY LAURENCE YEP

★ AmericanGirl®

For my niece, Franny, who went with me to The Nutcracker, *and to my wife, Joanne, who took me to Lincoln Center*

Published by American Girl Publishing
Copyright © 2014 American Girl

Questions or comments? Call 1-800-845-0005, visit **americangirl.com**, or write to Customer Service, American Girl, 8400 Fairway Place, Middleton, WI 53562-0497.

Printed in China
14 15 16 17 18 19 20 21 LEO 15 14 13 12 11 10 9 8

Illustrations by Anna Kmet

Special thanks to Kristy Callaway, executive director of Arts Schools Network; Shannon Gallagher, owner of and instructor at Premier Dance Academy, LLC, Madison, WI; and Angela Corosanite, founder and CEO of String Theory Schools

Photo credits: pp. 119–121, Dan Norman

Library of Congress Cataloging-in-Publication Data

Yep, Laurence, 1948–
Isabelle / by Laurence Yep ; illustrations by Anna Kmet.
    pages   cm
Summary: Isabelle, who attends a performing arts school in Washington, D.C., with her older sister, Jade, has a passion for ballet dancing but lacks self-confidence.
ISBN 978-1-60958-371-2 (pbk.) — ISBN 978-1-60958-427-6 (ebook)
1. Performing arts—Fiction. 2. Schools—Fiction. 3. Ballet dancing—Fiction. 4. Self-confidence—Fiction. 5. Sisters—Fiction.] I. Kmet, Anna, illustrator. II. Title.
PZ7.Y44Is 2014   [Fic]—dc23   2013041924

Contents

CHAPTER 1

Into the Studio

At my old school, a bus took us to a farm every autumn so that we could buy a pumpkin to carve. At my new school, the pumpkins had their revenge.

One minute I was talking to my friends as we walked through the school hallway. The next I was flat on my back with the taste of nylon in my mouth, staring up at a kid in an oversized pumpkin costume.

"Sorry, pumpkins always have the right-of-way," he insisted as he shuffled toward the drama department like an orange bulldozer. The hallway was crowded between classes, so students squeezed against one another to clear a path.

My friend Luisa was nine like me. She wore her dark brown hair pulled back in a bun. Though she was smaller than me, having a big brother had toughened her. Anger reddened the dark skin of her cheeks. "I thought vegetables had better manners!" she shouted.

"Cabbages do. Gourds don't," the boy joked as he swayed dangerously down the hall on two skinny, green-stockinged legs.

"Step out of that pumpkin suit and say that," Luisa snapped and started after him.

I grabbed her ankle as the pumpkin squeezed through the doorway of the drama studio. "Wait up,

Luisa," I said. "Don't get into a fight over me. What's gotten into you lately?"

Luisa seized my hands in hers and hauled me to my feet. She shrugged, brushing off my question. But then she finally said, "I'm just worried about my brother. He hasn't e-mailed me in like two weeks."

Luisa's older brother, Danny, had joined the army about six months ago. He was still in basic training at some military base in the South, but he wasn't very good about keeping in touch with her, and I could tell she really missed him. I tried to think of what it would be like if my big sister, Jade, wasn't around. And I knew there'd be a big empty hole inside me.

"Well, I'm still here," I said to Luisa, because it was all I could think of to say. "You can always talk to me."

"Thanks," Luisa said. She smiled and leaned over to nudge me gratefully.

The hallway had almost cleared of students, and suddenly the bell rang, signaling the start of the next period.

"Now we've got bigger problems than your brother. We're late for ballet," I groaned.

More than a hundred and fifty years ago,

this building had been a girls' academy. When Washington, D.C., converted it to a public school for the arts, a modern annex of concrete and steel was added, and the school was named after Anna Hart. She was a dancer who had become famous in New York and then had come home to create her own dance company—the Hart Dance Company, or HDC.

From far away in the building, violinists began warming up in the music room. Near us in the vocal arts room, voices warbled up and down the scales like robins on stair-climber machines.

Luisa started to trot down the corridor. Now that everyone else was in class, we could begin to run from the original building into the new annex, leaving the nineteenth century behind for the twenty-first. "Come on, Isabelle," she called to me.

"Coming," I said. I gave a skip and a hop and then ran after her. The music for my ballet routine began playing inside my head.

As I rounded another corner, I thought to myself, *I don't think I've stopped rushing since I got into Anna Hart.* Sometimes I was late because I was still getting lost in my new school. Other times it was because teachers were giving me extra instruction after class to bring me up to speed with the other students.

Isabelle

You couldn't miss the words still chiseled into the stones over the school entrance: *Per ardua ad astra.* It was the original girls' academy motto, and Jade told me that it was Latin for "Through difficulty, to the stars."

Teachers here at Anna Hart were determined to make sure that we all aimed high—and worked hard. My regular courses, such as English and math, were a lot tougher than at my old school. My modern dance and ballet classes were just as hard, and so were the classes in music, voice, and visual and theater arts. I knew, because I'd sat in on each of them during my first two weeks here. I wished there were thirty hours in a day so that I could take all of the arts, but I'd been allowed to sign up for only modern dance and ballet.

I'd been dying to get into Anna Hart ever since kindergarten, but there was a lottery for students from all of Washington, D.C. Even though I'd tried four-leaf clovers and crossing all my fingers and toes, I hadn't been lucky enough to win a spot, like Luisa.

My big sister, Jade, on the other hand, had gotten in on her very first try. She'd gone here from kindergarten to seventh grade and was twelve years old now. If ever a school and a student were meant for each other, it was Anna Hart and Jade.

A straight-A student, she was such an amazing dancer that the school even featured her picture on the web page for the ballet program.

If it hadn't been for Jade, I'd still be knocking on the front door of Anna Hart School of the Arts. But every year, the lottery allowed a few extra slots for the brothers and sisters of students. It had taken four years for my name to be chosen, but I was finally here.

Unfortunately, after a rough first month, I was beginning to think that coming here was the biggest mistake of my life.

As soon as we got to the ballet studio, Luisa and I plunged inside. Before I'd gotten into Anna Hart, I'd taken ballet three times a week at a pretty good dance academy. And I had learned all the moves, turns, and positions so well that I'd been one of the best dancers in my class.

That wasn't true here at Anna Hart, but the ballet studio still felt like my second home. I loved the soft whisper of cloth on floor as the other ballet students warmed up. They lay on their backs, stretching their arms and legs in ways that arms and legs didn't normally move. Some wore gray sweatshirts over their brightly colored leotards, as if pigeons and parrots were gathering together in the same birdbath.

Our teacher, Ms. Hawken, was a small, slim woman in a leotard with a crimson scarf tied around her waist. A matching ribbon circled her ponytail.

She didn't say anything to Luisa and me. She just nodded her head toward the girls' changing room. I was already wearing a purple leotard and dance skirt from modern dance class. And Luisa and I had put our hair in buns before modern dance, too, to save time now. I followed Luisa into the long, narrow changing room, where we stowed our bags in two empty lockers.

We made it back into the studio in time for warm-ups, and then Ms. Hawken sent us to the *barre*. Some kids found barre work boring, but I liked this part of class.

I moved a little slower than Luisa, so the only space left was at the end of the barre by Renata. She was a slender girl with dark brown hair that framed her narrow face. She was straightening her expensive leotard (which everyone *knew* was expensive because she had told us the price) as if it had to look perfect even for rehearsal.

At a nod from Ms. Hawken, Ms. Emile, the accompanist, began to play the piano in the corner. Standing sideways to the barre, I set my heels against each other with my toes pointed outward. Then I lowered my arms, curving them so that my fingertips pointed toward my legs.

"Demi-plié," Ms. Hawken said as I bent my legs and slowly squatted halfway down. Beneath me, the floor creaked and popped slightly. A tremor passed along the long barre as our many hands tugged at it, all at the same time.

"Keep your heels down, Stewart," Ms. Hawken reminded one of my classmates. She moved slowly along the line of students, adjusting an arm here, a leg there. "Bend your knees a little more, Madelyn. That's it."

Madelyn had transferred to Anna Hart this year, too, but she hadn't taken dance classes before, so she got extra attention from Ms. Hawken. Through her tights, I could see that her calf muscles were trembling.

Then our teacher said, "And now stretch. Not so fast, Luisa. You're not in a race. Slow, elegant."

As I rose carefully back to my original pose, I smiled at Luisa's reflection in the mirror, and she grinned back. My friend could do a lot of things, but "slow" would never be one of them.

Ms. Hawken led us through more arm and leg movements. Then Ms. Emile picked up the tempo, and Ms. Hawken said, "Now *battement fondu* forward."

My ballet slipper hissed along the floor as I swept my leg in a quick arc. I slid it front to back and side to side, pretending I was a bird sweeping the dust out of my nest with my wing. Ms. Hawken nodded her approval at me.

After a short while, she had us let go of the barre and move on to center work, a series of steps done across the floor.

"*Port de bras* the first," Ms. Hawken said. I loved how she rolled her *r*'s when she spoke French. It made what we were doing sound so elegant.

She demonstrated by raising her bent arms in front of her. As we followed along, she slowly raised her arms over her head, curling her fingertips toward one another. Then she lowered them, stretching both arms out to the sides and giving them a flutter before bringing them down and holding them in front of her again. "Now, port de bras the fifth," she instructed.

I began to lift my arms, but Ms. Hawken strode over to me with a little shake of her head. She placed her hand on my ribs and pressed. "Isabelle, keep your body still," she said. "Move just your arms."

It was so simple. And I'd done it so many times, I should've been able to do it in my sleep. But in our modern dance class, our teacher, Mr. Amici, had just told me that I was holding my body *too* stiffly. Modern dance used some of the same gestures as ballet, but it was as if my body had to learn a whole new language. In Ms. Hawken's class, I was having a refresher course in my original ballet language.

As Ms. Hawken called out instructions, I fell into the familiar routine of slowly stretching my muscles. It was soothing—even if my arms and legs were tired.

Sometimes when I looked into the mirror, I could imagine a long line of ballerinas extending beyond my reflection. The very same movements, the very same poses linked us in an unbroken chain that stretched back through the centuries. It made me feel as if I was part of something much bigger and more beautiful.

Yet I liked my modern dance class, too, because I got to move in different, fun ways. And some of the gestures and movements were brand-new to me. I didn't have to worry about doing exactly the same thing as a dancer had done three hundred years ago.

I could help create something fresh, and I liked that freedom.

Ms. Hawken said that many classical ballet companies were bringing in both modern and jazz choreographers, so it was good to learn many dance forms. I just had to juggle more stuff inside my head.

As Ms. Emile played the piano more quickly, Ms. Hawken took us through different short combinations of movements, building up to a series of jumps across the floor. *Jetés* were my all-time favorite part of ballet. I kicked my right leg out as I pushed off with my left. At the peak of my jump, I stretched my legs into a split. When I landed on my right leg, I bent it slightly and extended my left leg behind me. No wobbling.

The sun shone through the window, creating a shimmering path along the floor. All I had to do was follow it, feeling stronger and lighter with each leap. My feet thumped against the floor rhythmically along with my classmates' feet, sounding like distant drums.

I could have gone on jumping for the entire period, but finally the piano notes came to an end. Ms. Hawken clapped her hands. "Places, please," she said. "Time to be a bouquet."

Isabelle

Ms. Hawken had put tape down on the floor, outlining the shape and size of a stage. Renata and the other dancers moved eagerly to their spots on the floor to rehearse for the Autumn Festival. I lagged behind.

Every fall, students at Anna Hart put on a show for their parents. The teachers did the choreography and ran the tech, but the students made their own costumes—and the audience came in costume, too. For this year's show, our ballet class was doing a shortened version of "The Waltz of the Flowers."

Our modern dance class was performing, too—a pirate routine that Luisa was really excited about. But I had said no to being a pirate and yes to being a waltzing flower, because I thought the ballet routine would be easier for me. Boy, had I been wrong.

"Whenever you're ready, Isabelle," Ms. Hawken murmured.

Reluctantly, I walked toward the corner and took my spot, standing with the heel of one foot against the instep of the other.

My stomach began doing flip-flops. That had been happening more and more often. If there were such a thing as gymnastics for stomachs, mine would have won the gold medal for somersaulting.

Into the Studio

Ms. Hawken fiddled with her phone, and
French horns began to call from the studio speakers.
That's when my nightmare began.

CHAPTER 2

Dizzy Izzy

After two weeks of Ms. Hawken's patient coaching, I finally knew the choreography for our flower routine, but I always seemed to be one step behind everyone else. If I'd had a tail, Renata would have been stepping on it. As it was, I could smell her breath—maybe she had been chewing some cinnamon-flavored gum.

At one point in the choreography, the class was supposed to dance in two separate circles. Then we were each supposed to curl away from the circles and form two lines.

"Faster, Isabelle," Ms. Hawken called.

But when I tried to speed up, things seemed to get worse. I went left when I should have gone right. And during the rest of the routine, I often did the reverse of what everyone else was doing, going forward when I should have gone backward.

When it was over, Ms. Hawken gazed at the floor and then at me. "Isabelle, stay there," she said. "The rest of you take a break."

I could feel the blood rushing to my cheeks as the rest of the class began to sit on the floor and stretch. Madelyn smiled at me sympathetically. Since she was a beginner, Ms. Hawken had simplified her part of the routine so that she could handle it.

Did Ms. Hawken need to simplify mine, too? My cheeks burned hot.

"Let's try these steps again," Ms. Hawken suggested, demonstrating the series of steps she wanted to see.

I did my best to copy Ms. Hawken, but she frowned. "You're still a little off," she said. She began to snap her fingers rhythmically. "This tempo, Isabelle."

I tried again, but Ms. Hawken shook her head. "Still too slow," she said. She waved her hand toward a group of girls. "Renata, please show Isabelle."

Folding my arms, I stepped to the side. As Renata passed, she whispered, "Watch and learn, Dizzy Izzy."

I bit my lip, fighting the urge to say something mean back. All I could do was watch silently as Renata did my steps—perfectly.

It made me feel even worse when it was my turn again. I still couldn't do the steps fast enough.

Ms. Hawken motioned for me to sit in a corner. "Watch this time," she said. Then she took my spot in the lineup and began to dance with the others. "You're supposed to be here," she said. "Not still there," she added, pointing to another spot.

She called out a commentary like that throughout the rest of the waltz. Then she waved me over to join the other flowers. "Now, from the top."

I tried. I really did. I wanted to show everyone in the class that I belonged at Anna Hart, that I wasn't here just because of my sister.

Instead, I wallowed like a tugboat in a race with motorboats. And I just got worse and worse with each repetition. I was beginning to think I was never meant for ballet.

Renata got more and more disgusted with me. "It's hard to believe she's Jade's sister," she muttered to one of the other dancers.

I didn't try to defend myself—I was too frustrated with my own dancing—but Luisa said, "Shut up, Renata."

Ms. Hawken held up her hand to stop the dancing. Then she looked sternly at Renata and Luisa and said, "In my class, we treat everyone with respect. Got that?"

Luisa muttered an apology. Renata glared at me angrily as she mumbled, "Yes, ma'am." I think she blamed me for the reprimand.

Mercifully, the bell rang, ending the class. We did our *reverence*, girls curtsying with our arms in port de bras and boys bowing.

"Remember to bring your costumes next Thursday," Ms. Hawken said as we headed to the changing rooms.

Now that the narrow room was full of girls, there wasn't much space to walk. "Excuse me," I said.

No one budged, though. Maybe they blamed me for losing valuable rehearsal time, too.

"Leave this to me," Luisa said. Slipping in front of me, she began to elbow her way through the bodies ahead of us. I trailed in her wake, afraid to look any of the other dancers in the eye.

Once we had reached our bags at the very end of the room, Luisa changed into her regular clothes, but I took my time. I didn't want to have to leave with Renata and the others. When they were all gone, I finally zipped up my bag.

Luisa put her hand on my shoulder. "Don't let Renata get to you," she said, as if she could read my mind.

I shrugged, discouraged. "I don't know, Luisa," I said. "The first couple of weeks I was here, when the principal told me I should try the other arts classes, maybe she was trying to warn me to quit ballet."

Luisa shook her head. "No," she said firmly.

"If anyone was meant for ballet, it's you."

That's what I had always thought, too, but everything was so different here at Anna Hart. At least I had my good friend Luisa in my corner.

As we finally were leaving the dressing room, Ms. Hawken gave me an encouraging smile. "Isabelle, you've got all the skills, and you know the steps of your routine," she said. "You've just got to have confidence in yourself. You're so afraid of making a mistake that your brain and your body keep getting their signals crossed."

I nodded, but I wasn't sure what to do with that information. "How exactly do I get that kind of confidence?" I asked.

Ms. Hawken stroked the knot on her scarf. "I was wearing this when I auditioned for the HDC," she said. "It's my lucky charm. Even though it's only a silly superstition, I still wear it when I try out for a big part. A lot of dancers have lucky charms like this."

Luisa spoke up from beside me. "You don't really believe the scarf is magical, do you?" she asked skeptically.

"Not really," said Ms. Hawken. "But it does trick my mind a little so that it stops worrying about flubbing and lets my body do what I've trained it to do. Maybe you should find your own charm, Isabelle."

At this point, I was willing to try anything.

On the bus ride home, I thought about Ms. Hawken's scarf and wondered how I could wear something like that with my own dance costume. I had to wait until Mom got home from work to really figure it out, because it was Mom who was going to design and sew our outfits for the Autumn Festival.

I ambushed her as soon as she got in the door. "Mom, could my Autumn Festival outfit have a scarf?" I asked her.

Mom looked guilty as she took off her coat and hung it up. "I haven't had time to design it yet," she admitted, "so you can have as many scarves as you want." As she pulled a clip out of her long brown hair and shook it free, she added, "But I'm glad you're getting your own ideas about what you want. Maybe *you* should design the costumes for yourself and Jade this year."

"Me?" I asked, stunned. "But you're the expert."

Mom smiled. "You're always asking me

questions when I bring work home," she said. "By now, you've soaked up centuries of the best designs."

Mom worked at the Smithsonian conserving old textiles, taking apart and repairing gowns that were sometimes two hundred years old. I'd seen everything that she used to study antique clothing—from photos and X-rays to microscopic close-ups. And it was true—I always was asking Mom questions, because she always had interesting answers.

"I really think you can do this, Isabelle," Mom said as she walked into the kitchen to start dinner. "Just try it and see what you think."

So I went into the living room, where I had dumped my backpack. Getting out my tablet and a stylus, I sat on the sofa to sketch out some designs.

From our bedroom overhead, I kept hearing the same excerpt from *Carmen*. Jade and her classmates were dressing up as gypsies for the Autumn Festival. Jade's dancing feet made faint noises as I began to draw on the tablet. After starting over a few times, I finally sketched out a gypsy costume that I thought Jade would like.

But it was harder when it came to designing my own. I knew I wanted a scarf or sash that might bring me luck, like Ms. Hawken's, but I wasn't sure about anything else.

While I thought, I stared at the mobile—something Mom had made—that hung from the middle of the living-room ceiling. At work, Mom had to follow rigid rules and exact patterns as she reassembled old clothing. But in her personal time, she combined pieces of clothing with other fabrics and shapes to create mobiles and wall hangings. Each design was unique—and all her own.

Mom called this mobile "Pond Dreams." Its pieces were so well balanced that just entering the room would make them stir. Its colors and shapes kept changing before my eyes and forming new patterns, like a kaleidoscope.

Mom had created it two summers ago after our family had visited the Aquatic Gardens at Kenilworth Park. It had just rained, and round lily pads covered the pond like shining green scales, with water lilies and lotuses scattered among them like jewels. The water was so still that it mirrored the sky, and the reflections of clouds seemed to glide dreamily among the plants. It reminded me of the Claude Monet painting we had just seen in a special show at the National Gallery.

I had gazed at one particular flower floating

among the broad green leaves. The pointed outer petals were pink and the inner ones yellow, deepening to gold near the center. Covered in raindrops, the petals looked like slices cut from beautiful stones.

I tried to see the stem of the flower, but the water was too murky.

"How tall are the water lilies?" I'd asked.

"They're quite tall, but we see only their tops," said Mom, pointing to the water below. "Their roots are all the way down in the mud."

"How can such pretty flowers grow in such dirty water?" Jade had asked.

"The water's cloudy because it's full of food for the plants," Mom explained. "If you were a lily, living in a pond would be like living on a buffet table."

When a sudden gust of wind blew across the pond, the flowers bowed their heads—as if a giant hand were petting them. The clouds reflected in the water dissolved in ripples that began to race across the pond. The leaves dipped and rose like bucking horses, and the flowers began to whirl in small circles, still bound by their stems. The pink-and-yellow flower must have had a longer stem, because it moved in a much larger, more restless circle.

Then a gap opened in the drifting clouds, and

a small patch of sunlight seemed to stroll through the park. When it reached the pond, the raindrops on the flowers and lily pads began to glitter like diamonds.

The wind must have snapped the stem of my favorite water lily, because it spun through the leaves and across the pond, bobbing as it coasted over each mini wave. And then it was gone.

Mom seemed as taken by the lilies as I was, because as soon as we got home, she had begun to work on ideas for a new mobile. And over the next few months, anything woven or spun became the raw material for her artwork. Jade and I played our own small part by finding scraps of sheer fabric, tulle, and lace at thrift stores, flea markets, and rummage sales.

Bit by bit, Mom had mounted the different fabrics on wire frames. Then she had hung each portion on a wire connected to the ceiling in the living room, until she had created what looked like a single water lily among many green lily pads and clouds and rippling water. Here and there, tiny crystals flashed like raindrops in the sun.

That pond had been really good luck for us. It had inspired Mom to make this beautiful work of art. Now that pond was helping to inspire my designs—and my dancing.

Isabelle

I drew eagerly on my tablet. My sash would have flowers on it. Yes, I wanted a really, really long sash so that the flowers would swirl around me as I danced. The thoughts came even faster than I could draw, and as I worked, a smile spread slowly across my face.

I'd show Renata who Dizzy Izzy *really* was.

When I felt someone patting my shoulder the next morning, I thought it was our kitten, Tutu. She'd been a birthday gift to Mom in May, but Tutu preferred sleeping in Jade's and my room. Mom blamed it on Dad's snoring.

Tutu had been such a cute little white cotton ball in the shelter, but she turned out to be a real furry handful. Normally a kitten might wake you with loud meowing. But Tutu preferred to hop on top of you and stroll up and down your spine. When Jade or I would finally sit up, Tutu would jump off and twitch her whiskers in surprise, as if to say, *Oh, was that your back? I thought you were the hallway rug.* And just as she had planned, one of us would feed her and then play with her.

Lately, though, Tutu spent most of her time with Jade—maybe because my sister was always sneaking her little treats. I sighed, just thinking about it. *Jade is a better dancer than I am. Jade is a better student than I am. And now even our kitten likes her better than me. Sometimes life just isn't fair.*

I tried to push Tutu off me. "Go bother Jade, will you, Tutu?" I murmured sleepily.

But it was Mom looking down at me through her glasses. She'd pulled her pale brown hair behind her in a ponytail. "Come on, sleepyhead," she said. "We want to get to the flea market before all the good stuff for your costumes gets snapped up. If we hurry, we can get our shopping done and still listen to your dad's band play."

I poked my head out from under the quilt. Jade's bed was empty, but then she always got up earlier than I did. "Flea market?" I asked with a yawn. "What about school?"

"It's Saturday, honey," said Mom, gently brushing the hair away from my face. "So get dressed. There's a bus in twenty minutes."

My family tried to do things together every Saturday. If we weren't heading to a rummage sale or our favorite thrift stores to hunt for stuff for Mom's art, we were catching a matinee at the Kennedy Center or heading down to some event on the National Mall or visiting a museum—Washington seems to have a museum for everything. Finding something to do was never a problem.

Jade came into our room, nibbling on a sliced bagel. She was already dressed in capris and a blouse. Her long blonde hair hung down past her shoulders, held neatly away from her face by a light blue barrette. Tutu trotted at her heels.

"What do you want on your bagel, Isabelle?" Jade asked.

"I . . . uh . . ." It was hard to string thoughts together, let alone words. I had stayed up late sketching on my tablet. It wasn't until almost eleven that I'd finally come up with an outfit design that I liked. By then, though, Jade had already been asleep, with Tutu resting next to her.

I felt like closing my eyes again, but I couldn't resist the smell of a freshly toasted bagel. "Stuff," was all I could say.

Jade was an expert at Isabelle-ese. "Gotcha," she said. "Jelly with cream cheese."

"*Me-owr?*" Tutu flicked an inquiring ear at my sister.

"I already fed you," Jade scolded. When Tutu rubbed against Jade's calf, though, my sister relented. "Okay," she said. "Maybe one little snack."

As Jade turned back toward the kitchen, she rose on her right foot, extended her left leg almost parallel to the floor, spun in place, and then stepped over Tutu. Jade made it look so easy. Dancing came as naturally to her as breathing.

Then Jade high-stepped out of the room, arching each foot in a perfect curve with every step.

She was often complimented on her "banana feet," which is a good thing to have if you are a ballerina. As Jade walked, Tutu wove back and forth between her ankles, picking up and lowering her paws like a ballerina *en pointe*. It was almost as if the two of them were performing a *pas de deux*.

My throat caught a little as it sometimes did when I saw Jade dance. She was so graceful in everything she did—whether she was performing a ballet step, striking a pose, or just teasing our kitten. Even with all the lucky charms in the world, I'd *never* be that graceful.

Mom misunderstood my silence. She ran her fingers through my hair like a comb, taking out the snags. "You look tired, honey," she said. "Are you worried you won't get into *The Nutcracker*?"

Several weekends ago, the HDC had held auditions for its holiday show, *The Nutcracker*. Jade had suggested we both try out for the show. I didn't think I had any chance to get in, but I'd gone with her and Luisa to keep them company.

I forced myself to wake up now. "There's no way I'm going to be chosen for *The Nutcracker*," I said.

"You don't know that," Mom replied as she pulled a pair of capris from my closet. "You were good. And since there are three casts, you've got three times as many chances to get a role."

Six evening shows and three matinees each week would wreck even the strongest dancers, so different casts would take turns performing. Mom was right—having three casts for the show did improve my chances.

"But I wasn't as good as a lot of other dancers," I said, thinking of Renata—who had unfortunately auditioned for *The Nutcracker,* too. I slowly pulled off my purple pajamas. Then I opened my dresser drawer and pulled out my lucky coral shirt with the dancer design on the front.

"You were good like *you,*" Mom insisted as I tugged the shirt over my head. She sat on the bed while I pulled on the capris, too. "When you were a baby, it was like you were full of dance juice. You were always kicking your legs, so we could never keep you covered up with a blanket. And when you were two, you'd leap around whenever you heard music. We had to put everything breakable out of reach."

I quickly brushed my hair. "I know," I said. "I've seen the photo."

There was a picture of Dad and me from when I was small. I was just a blur in it, my face hidden in a whirlwind of hair as I turned away from the camera. Poor Dad was standing up, holding his laptop on one palm while he worked on it with his free hand. He hadn't dared to set it on the coffee table because it would have been in range of my kicking feet.

I checked the mirror. My hair was as blonde as Jade's, but I decided it needed something a little extra exciting that morning. So I picked up some pink hair extensions. I tried them in several different places before I settled on the right spots, and Mom helped me put them in.

Mom held up some sneakers, but I shook my head and reached for my glittery silver and gold sling-back shoes. Finally, to show everyone that I meant business, I shrugged into my black jacket.

"What do you think?" I asked Mom, inspecting myself in the mirror again.

Mom's reflection appeared behind me as she studied me. Then she nodded her approval. "Very nice, very creative. Very you. You've got a good eye for style," she said. "But then, you insisted on choosing your own clothes almost as soon as you could walk."

I grinned. "Sorry that I was such a brat back then," I said. "I mean, not just about the clothes but about the dancing."

Mom hugged me from behind. I felt her laughter as well as heard it. "Don't be," she said. "You said you had wings and were flying."

I studied my outfit from all angles in the mirror. It *was* a great outfit, and it made me feel as if I could handle anything. I slipped off my shoes and spun in a graceful pirouette, watching my room and Mom whirl past my eyes. I took a couple more steps and then launched into a leap, my arms spread like a sail catching the wind. For a moment, I felt like I was floating.

When I landed on Jade's bed, Mom warned, "Better not let Jade catch you."

But I was brimming over with that dance juice Mom had talked about. I couldn't stop moving my arms and legs. So I hopped along the bed, kicking up my feet as I went.

Lunging forward, Mom caught me around the waist and, with a laugh, swung me back down to the floor. "Make up Jade's bed again before she sees what you did to it, okay?" she scolded.

I kept dancing as I straightened the covers. It was great to dance just for the fun of it. *If only I could feel like this when I'm a waltzing flower, too,* I thought as I smoothed the last crease from the bed.

I finished my bagel as we stepped out the door and onto the stoop. We lived on the edge of George-town, about as far southeast as you can get and still be in the district. Dad's grandparents had bought our house a long time ago, but Dad said the street looked pretty much the same then as it did now: with lots of cozy little two-story brick homes squeezed together like lines of dancers dressed in warm, red wool.

All around me were the usual signs of autumn. A strong wind last night had shaken down lots of leaves from tall gingko trees, some as old as the homes around them. I could barely see the diagonal pattern of the brick sidewalk for all the yellow, fan-shaped leaves. On one bare branch, a wood thrush sang a last farewell song before leaving for the winter. A squirrel, fat from summer meals, was waddling around search-ing for last-minute snacks.

As we walked quickly down the sidewalk, I wondered how I could capture autumn in a dance routine. How would I turn the thrush's song and the squirrel's hunt into steps?

Mom urged me along to catch the waiting bus. When we stepped onboard, Mom showed the driver her bus pass, and Jade and I showed our student passes. I rode this same public bus to school five days a week. We found seats about midway down the aisle. Mom sat beside me, and Jade took a seat behind us.

"Let's see your designs," Mom said, so I pulled my tablet from my backpack and handed it to her.

She was so busy examining my designs that she barely noticed as the bus crossed 35th Street. But both Jade and I swiveled our heads to look a couple of blocks north toward Helen Tischler, the performing arts high school. Jade was bound to go there, but this was probably as close as I was going to get.

The bus turned south, skirting the edge of the Georgetown University campus. We saw only a few students scattered around the stately old brick buildings. Mom never looked up. She was still examining my designs.

The longer Mom didn't say anything, the more anxious I got. Finally, I couldn't take it any longer. "If you don't think they're any good—" I said.

"I think they're excellent," Mom said. Turning, she held out the tablet to my sister. "What do you think of your gypsy outfit, Jade?"

Jade was tugging at her sweatshirt sleeve. She looked up with a start. "Sorry . . . what?" she said.

"Why are you fidgeting?" Mom asked, staring at the sweatshirt. It didn't quite cover the cuff of Jade's lavender blouse. "Jade, have you grown a little?"

Jade shook her head. "No," she said quickly, and then, as if to change the subject, she leaned forward to inspect my designs.

I waited, hoping for some praise from Jade. Instead, what I got was a shrug. "The gypsy's okay," Jade murmured, but then she tapped the design for my costume. "Isabelle, you should make the sash for your outfit a little shorter."

"It has to be *long*," I insisted. "It's the most important part of my costume."

Jade wouldn't let up, though. "It could be hard to dance with something that long," she said again. Sometimes my big sister went too far and tried to bully me into what she thought was right.

I crossed my arms. Jade could think what she liked about her outfit, but she couldn't pick on mine. After all, Jade never asked about Mom's work the way I did. So my sister wouldn't know as much about design as I did. Was Jade jealous because I was finally better at something than she was?

"Mom says my costume is fine. I'm not going to change a thing," I insisted stubbornly.

"But—" Jade began to protest.

"No means no," I snapped.

Jade folded her arms, too, and slammed back against her seat. "Suit yourself."

CHAPTER 4

Flea-Market Magic

Thornton Landing stood at the foot of the Francis Scott Key Bridge, where cars and trucks thumped rhythmically overhead. Behind it, more vehicles sped along the elevated highway. Once, boats had crossed the Potomac River to this spot, but now a restaurant and shops lined the riverbank.

There were several sculls on the river. The small, narrow rowing boats skimmed over the surface like water bugs. Farther to the southwest, just peeking around Theodore Roosevelt Island, were the curving Watergate Apartments and the Kennedy Center, where we often went to see shows and concerts.

The owners of Thornton Landing held a monthly flea market. Today the market was already crowded, though it had been open for only an hour. The sun was shining and the air was warm—sixty degrees or so—the perfect weather for treasure hunting.

Jade may not have liked my design for my costume, but she perked right up when it was time to shop with Mom and me. We'd been at the market for just ten minutes when we found half a roll of fine white tulle that had been used as plant netting in a garden. From another stall, we got a long strip of

cloth with colorful designs and some silk flowers
to sew onto it. They would make the perfect sash.
I could already feel the luck in them.

For Jade, we got a peasant blouse and skirt
that Mom would embellish and big hoop earrings.
From another dealer, we bought a lace-edged tablecloth for really cheap—after I pointed out to the
dealer the many coffee stains that made it look like
a leopard skin. Mom said she could cut it and dye it
to make a shawl for Jade's gypsy costume. She had
a bunch of tiny tassels at home that she could attach
to the hem, too.

In return for my helping to find things for her
costume, Jade found me a black cuff bracelet to match
the unitard I was going to wear, plus a tiara.

We were both tempted by the poster of Jackie
Sanchez. She was Jade's and my favorite dancer. Not
only had she gone to Anna Hart like us, but she was
now one of the principal dancers at New York City
Ballet. We'd actually gotten to see her last year when
the company came through Washington. Even though
we had seen her only at a distance, from way up in
the second balcony, it still had been a thrill.

Instead of the poster, I bought a postcard of
Jackie, which Jade let me have after I won a game of

rock-paper-scissors. I hoped it was a sign that my luck was changing.

After glancing at her watch, Mom smiled with satisfaction. "Well, I think we had a pretty good day," she said. "We not only got the stuff for your costumes but for your dad's and mine as well."

Mom and Dad would dress up for the Autumn Festival, too—it was tradition that the audience come in costume.

"Want to grab a *fatira* and then listen to your dad's band?" Mom asked.

Fatira were yummy fried pancakes that we often bought from an Ethiopian food stall. We were heading toward the stall when I heard a man say, "Ain't no such thing as magic."

The dark-skinned man was over six feet tall and almost as broad. He looked as if he was in his twenties and was wearing a Washington Wizards basketball team jacket that had enough material to cover an easy chair. So at first I didn't see who he was talking to.

"But there really is magic, friend." I recognized that voice. It belonged to my friend and classmate Gabriel.

The man smiled in a superior way. "Can't fool

me," he said. "Magic is all mirrors and stuff."

Gabriel's older sister, Zama, was standing a few feet away. She winked at me when she saw us.

Zama's curly hair had been pulled up and bound above her head like a kind of crown. She was carefully eating French fries dripping with mumbo sauce—sort of a mix of sweet-and-sour with barbecue sauce.

I circled around the man so that I could see Gabriel. He was a tall African American boy with curly hair, and he was grinning at the man in his usual friendly way. The acting lessons Gabriel took at school really helped his magic act. He pulled back his sleeves now to expose his bare forearms. "No mirrors, no stuff here," he said. He pulled a deck of cards from his pocket. "Just my fifty-two friends making miracles."

When the man folded his arms skeptically, Gabriel added, "Or are you scared to find out there really is magic?"

The man gave a snort and eased a single card from the deck's middle. Holding it so that Gabriel couldn't see it, the man showed it to his friends, but I saw that it was a four of spades.

"Now picture it in your mind," Gabriel said

and closed his eyes. He paused for a long moment. "Sorry. I'm new at magic. Can you think a little bit harder?"

The man leaned over and jabbed his fingers rhythmically at Gabriel, as if they were shoving his thoughts into Gabriel's brain.

Gabriel pretended to stagger back, and his eyes popped open. "Whoo-ee," he said. "So much brain power." He rubbed his forehead as if he had a headache. "Now put the card back in the deck, please."

The man stuck the card halfway into the deck in Gabriel's hand and then used his fingers to tap it in the rest of the way.

Gabriel arched an eyebrow. "You keeping an eye on me?" he asked.

The man pointed at his three friends and then at himself. "Eight eagle eyes," he said.

"Then you ought to be able to tell me how I did this," said Gabriel as he fanned out the cards with their backs showing. Only the four of spades was faceup.

The man laughed in delight, along with his friends. "I didn't see nothing. Did you?" he asked. When they shook their heads, the man leaned forward, arms swinging loose by his sides. "Do another."

He might have been over six feet tall, but he sounded as excited as a six-year-old.

Before Gabriel could begin a new trick, Zama called, "Got to go, Gabe." She played bass in Dad's band and needed to start setting up for the show.

"Sorry, guys," said Gabriel with a shrug. "I've got something important to do. But if you're still around afterward, I'll show you some more magic."

Looking genuinely disappointed, the man raised a hand. "Okay, then," he said. "Later, Magic Man."

As the four of us headed off together, Jade leaned in toward Gabriel and asked, "So, how did you do it?"

He frowned with mock sternness and then said, "You know a magician never tells his secrets."

"Not even to a friend?" I coaxed.

"Well, I can tell you this much," said Gabriel. "I get people to see what I want them to see." When he saw my disappointed look, he added, "If you really want to know, go to Shaka's Magic Shop. Ask for the pamphlet on the deck flip."

"Is that where you learned how to do magic?" Mom asked him.

"Shaka's an old friend of our grandmom,"

explained Zama. She squeezed Gabriel's shoulders and said, "I usually take this boy down there to keep him out of trouble."

While we were waiting in line by the Axum food van for our fatira, I could hear the sound of drums as Dad began his sound check.

Gabriel put his card deck away, but he was wriggling his fingers in one of his strengthening exercises. "The first time Shaka performed magic, I was as blown away as those guys today," he said. "I wanted to make other people feel the same way."

"Like little kids at Christmas?" I asked.

Gabriel scratched his head. "It's better than that," he said. "Your brain's telling you one thing and your eyes are telling you another. So it ought to upset you. But instead you feel good." He tapped the side of his head. "Because if your brain can be wrong about the cards, maybe it's wrong about other stuff. Maybe wishes can come true—like that guy could be a professional basketball player, if he wanted to be, and play for the Wizards."

And I thought, *And maybe a klutz like me could even learn how to dance.*

If only magic were real.

A jazz club, Owl Lane, had sponsored the music stage, which was a platform about thirty feet square. Dad was already leaning over his drum kit. He was wearing his favorite bright red T-shirt. Luisa's father—whom Jade and I call Uncle Davi—was there, too, playing his guitar during a sound check. He was a short man with wavy brown shoulder-length hair and a mustache.

The band's drums and guitar cases were on-stage between the portable speakers. Luisa was taking CDs from a cardboard box and laying them out on a small table to the side of the stage. Up until now, her brother, Danny, had been in charge of selling the CDs, but Luisa had taken his place.

I gathered the food trash from the others and dumped it into the garbage can. Then I walked over toward Luisa. "Need a hand?" I asked.

"Almost finished," she answered, adjusting a CD on a stack that already looked pretty even. "Danny used to just dump them on the table."

I straightened another stack of CDs. "How is Danny doing?" I asked.

"Who knows?" said Luisa without looking up. "Still no texts or e-mails. It's like he forgot all about me." She couldn't keep the hurt from her voice.

I got out my phone. "Smile," I said, snapping a picture. I sent it to Luisa's phone and said, "Maybe this'll make him homesick enough to call you."

Luisa took out her own phone. "At least, it'll show him what a display *should* look like," she said. But the corners of her mouth turned up as her thumbs danced out a message to Danny.

Uncle Davi stopped playing to wave Zama up onstage. "Don't keep our fans waiting," he called with a wink. At the moment, we were the only "fans" near the stage.

With a shrill, happy cry, Zama began shaking her hips and pumping her fists to the beat of Dad's drum. She danced up the steps and across the stage to her bass guitar. After she had slung it around her neck and tried a few chords, she nodded to Uncle Davi.

Finally, Uncle Davi stepped up to the microphone and turned it on. *"Bom dia! Bom dia!"* he shouted. That was Brazilian Portuguese for good morning. "Everyone enjoying the day so far?" His voice thundered through the flea market. Because of the traffic from the bridge and the freeway, the sound had been turned up.

Beside us, about a dozen people had started to gather, either munching their breakfast or taking a break from shopping. But Mom, Jade, Gabriel, Luisa, and I were the only ones to call out, "Yes-s-s!"

Uncle Davi motioned to his ear. "Can't hear, can't hear," he said. Then he repeated himself: "Enjoying the day?"

This time more people joined in with us.

"Well, your day is going to get ee-ven better!" Uncle Davi predicted.

Dad raised his drumsticks and began tapping out the beat. With the rhythm fixed in their heads, all three musicians launched into a cover version of an old rock song. Uncle Davi spread his legs in a wide stance and arched his back as he played, and Zama was wagging her head from side to side. But I almost didn't recognize the madman twisting and flailing behind the drums and cymbals.

Dad was a hospital administrator, but next to us, jazz was his real love. He not only played the drums but also did all the band's arrangements and composed new songs.

Though the band loved jazz, they were good

enough to play almost anything. So they were always in demand for weddings, bar and bat mitzvahs, and other festivals in the city. At a noisy public event like the flea market, Dad liked to start with loud, lively, familiar tunes to draw a crowd.

By the end of the second song, the band had drawn about thirty listeners. Uncle Davi took the microphone from the stand and walked over to Dad.

Nerves made Dad's voice rise a little. "I've written a little jazz number for my wife, who inspires me every day," he said, pointing a drumstick toward Mom. "My wife, Nancy."

Jade and I both turned in delight toward Mom. Her cheeks reddened as a few people clapped along with us. Dad waited until the applause was done and then added, "It's called 'Pond Dreams,' after one of her masterpieces."

I turned to Mom at the same time Jade did. "Did you know?" I asked.

Mom had paused with her palms together in mid-clap. "No," she said with an excited little laugh.

Dad's version of "Pond Dreams" began with the slow, dreamy notes of an old song that my third-grade class used to sing:

"Sweet and low, sweet and low,
Wind of the western sea . . ."

Then the band started to play with the familiar tune, just as Mom might with a piece of lace. In
her hands, an ordinary lacy collar could become an
angel's wing, an icy pond, or the moon in one of her
fabric creations.

As the song flowed around me, it swept me
back to that pond. The burst of sunlight had been so
bright and hot on my face. And then the cool breeze
had blown across the water, and the water lily had
broken free.

I felt like . . . like . . . Images and memories
and emotions flooded into my mind faster and faster,
piling up inside. But I wasn't a poet. I didn't have the
words. And I wasn't an artist, so I couldn't paint a
picture.

I was a dancer.

My body would tell the world how wonderful
I thought it was. My arms and legs began to move on
their own as my feelings flowed into them.

Jade couldn't resist, either. She held out her
hand to me. We ran together to the space in front of
the stage.

Luisa saw us dancing, and she raced to join us, too. When I grasped her hand, I thought her palm tingled with electricity. Then, whipping her arms over her head, Luisa started to move. She must have had all this energy locked up inside. It was like trying to dance with a lightning bolt. At first, I didn't see how I could keep up with her, but then she grinned at me and said, "Come on! Dance, girl!"

It was as if some of the electricity shot from her into me. At first, I followed her lead, circling my arms above my head and kicking a leg out and around. Then, after a while, I ended the arm motion with a flick of my wrists and ankles. Instantly, Luisa picked up the move and did the same. But when she per- formed her move, it seemed as if a super motor was whirling her wrist around.

While Jade danced closer to the band, Luisa and I went back and forth like that. One of us would copy the other until someone added a little twist. And that would take us into new steps and motions. It was like the way Dad, Uncle Davi, and Zama would toss the lead back and forth to one another in the song.

And then we weren't dancers and musicians performing separately in our own little worlds any- more. Instead, we were all creating the same dance and music together. As I danced, I felt free, light, and happy—just as I had when I was small.

From the stage, Uncle Davi shouted encouragement: *"Bom, bom."*

When Luisa saw a customer with the band's CD in one hand and his wallet in the other, she danced over to wait on him. And then it was just Jade and me again.

Jade swayed over beside me and began imitating my moves, just as Luisa had. But when Jade kicked out her leg, it wasn't just energetic, like mine. It was longer, leaner, higher—and somehow more graceful, too.

Suddenly, my body felt heavy—my moves stiff and clumsy compared to those of my sister. I felt as if I were wearing lead shoes and mittens. I was glad when the song ended and I could step away and sit on the edge of the stage.

When the music started up again, Luisa waved me toward the dance area, but I shook my head. I just didn't feel like dancing anymore, at least not until I could wear my new costume with the long sash—my lucky charm. I sure hoped it would give me the confidence I needed.

Mom was still humming Dad's tune when we went into her sewing room at home. Dad had found a song in that pond. Now it was my turn to be inspired by it, too.

I was so eager to get started on our costumes that I didn't notice Tutu slip into the sewing room behind us. But Jade alertly dropped her bag and scooped up our kitten. "No, you don't, you bad girl," she scolded affectionately.

For Tutu, Mom's sewing room was a paradise of delights crying out to be torn up.

"*Me-owr*," Tutu protested, kicking her legs and wiggling in Jade's grasp, but my sister deposited our kitten in the hallway and closed the door before Tutu could dart back inside.

Then Mom got out her sewing kit. It was an old carved wooden box that had belonged to her grandmother.

It was hard to believe that Mom created such beautiful artwork in this pack-rat's nest. The metal shelves that reached from floor to ceiling were over-flowing with bolts of fabric and plastic bins full of scraps. Old clothes and tablecloths were piled high on the floor, ready to be cut up for her art.

Though I saw Henrietta, Mom's trusty old

sewing machine, I almost didn't recognize the table it sat on. For one thing, I could actually see the tabletop instead of mounds of fabric scraps and half-finished pieces. I pointed at a green cutting mat with its grid of white lines. "When did you get the mat?" I asked.

"It's always been there," Mom said, grinning. "You just never noticed it before." She got out her measuring tape. "I think I already know your measurements, Isabelle, but let's make sure."

My measurements were the same as usual, but when Mom tried to take Jade's, my sister held up her hands. "You don't need them," she insisted. "We've already got everything we need for my outfit."

"Put on the blouse anyway," Mom urged.

"It'll fit fine," said Jade, tilting forward to pull the blouse over her head.

When she straightened up, though, we saw that the blouse was too short, exposing an inch of my sister's stomach. Jade gave a little grunt as she tried to pull it lower but couldn't.

"Hmm," Mom said. "I really think you've grown a little."

"I'm just the same height as always," Jade insisted. "You know a size small can be different from shirt to shirt."

"That's true," Mom admitted as she scratched the side of her head. "I should've had you try it on before we bought it. But I wanted to make sure we got to the stage on time."

Jade hunched her shoulders and began chewing her lip, and I figured she was upset over the blouse. So I tried to think of a way to make it better. Then I had a brainstorm.

I yanked the tablecloth out of a bag. "I bet there's enough material here to make a sash as well as a shawl for you, Jade," I said. "That'll cover up your waist."

Jade looked at me gratefully before she began taking off the blouse. "There, you see?" she said to Mom. "Problem solved."

Whenever I spent time in Mom's sewing room, I forgot about my troubles. I just relaxed and enjoyed the rhythmic sweep of my arm as I sent the needle in and out of the cloth.

"You're almost as good with a needle as Mom," Jade said, watching me work.

"No one's as good as she is," I insisted.

"You've got a talent for the needle, Isabelle,"

Mom agreed as she stitched small tassels to the bottom of Jade's shawl.

That meant a lot to me, coming from Mom. Looking up, I said, "Thanks." But I didn't go back to sewing right away. Instead, I watched Mom's arm, moving back and forth as she worked on my skirt. Her eyebrows wrinkled together in concentration, but she had a peaceful little smile on her face. Mom was as happy when she had a needle in her hand as I was.

Then I caught Jade gazing at Mom and me. "I love it here in the sewing room," she said with a little sigh. "Sometimes I wish we could hide out in here forever."

Mom finished tying off a thread. "Hide from what, honey?" she asked, reaching for a pair of scissors.

Jade just shrugged. Dipping her head, she went back to sewing.

Who knew that the time we'd spent in the sewing room would help me in modern dance class two days later? But it did.

"This is *not* dance!" Mr. Amici had just said

as he ran around like crazy, waving his arms in the air and wagging his head from side to side with his tongue sticking out.

He was a short man with black hair who must have really liked the color black, because I never saw him wear anything else. Today he was in a black T-shirt and yoga pants with a matching wool cap and shoes. Except for his pink face and arms, he looked like a giant felt-tip marker.

"You should have a reason for everything you do," he said. "So *visualize*. Have a clear image in your head for each motion. And when you dance, move from image to image." He set both index fingers on his forehead. "So, everybody, picture in your mind a common household object."

What should I imagine? A shopping bag? A bagel?

Luisa caught my eye and shrugged her shoulders. She didn't know what to do, and neither did I.

Mr. Amici lowered his hands. "Now dance," he instructed, "imagining that you're doing something with that object."

I was afraid Mr. Amici would call on me, so I stepped backward to hide behind my classmates. That made me think of Jade hiding out in Mom's

56

sewing room. Jade was right about that room—I felt safe there, too. Suddenly that gave me an idea.

I was ready when Mr. Amici gestured to me. "Isabelle, what do you have for us?" he asked.

After walking to the center of the room, I slowly bowed my head and started to sew with an invisible needle. Gradually, I began to smile as peacefully as Mom did whenever she held a sewing needle in her hand.

It just seemed natural to let my arm weave back and forth, more and more widely until it was swinging rhythmically like a pendulum in a grandfather clock. I felt so relaxed that it was easy to keep the peaceful expression on my face. Before I knew it, my whole body was swaying along with my arm. I wished my hair hadn't been in a bun, because it would have been nice to have the strands swish around, too.

The rocking motion made it impossible to stay in one place. Instead it swept me gently across the floor. It was as if I had *become* the needle now, stitching one side of the floor to the other with invisible thread. I finished by twisting my body round and round, as if I were tying a knot.

When I was done, Mr. Amici tapped a finger against his chin. "Excellent, Isabelle," he said. "You made it clear that you were sewing before you translated that action into something else. More importantly, you made me feel as calm and happy as you were."

I felt like a dancer again as I left modern dance class for ballet. Maybe I was finally getting the hang of my dance classes here at Anna Hart.

My good mood lasted through the barre and center work in ballet class, and even into the start of our flower routine. I was actually doing the steps on time! As my arms and legs moved to the music, I began to enjoy myself, just as I used to at my old dance academy.

But then I remembered that a tricky part was coming up. I became so anxious to do it right that I rushed and curved away from the line of flowers too early. I pulled up just in time before colliding with Stewart.

As gracefully as I could, I stepped back to my proper place. But by then, my confidence had gone down the drain, and I found myself falling farther and farther behind the others. I held on tight to the image of my costume in my mind. I just needed that lucky sash to work.

That night, at home, Jade and I worked on our costumes. We worked on them the next night, too. Mom did all the fancy sewing, but Jade and I helped her baste some of the pieces together by sewing long, loose stitches. We also sewed the simpler seams on the machine.

On Wednesday evening, I got to try on my costume for the first time. Mom had outdone herself dyeing and spray-painting the tulle skirt. The gold, yellow, and pink layers surrounded me like the petals of my favorite water lily. We dyed a pair of ballet shoes, too, and stitched on long ribbons. I crisscrossed them around my ankles.

When I finally tied the flower sash around my waist, it was everything I'd hoped it would be. But would it help me dance better? When I pirouetted, the tulle skirt belled up and the sash floated like a wing of flowers around me. I felt as light as a dandelion seed. I began to hum the waltz, and without thinking, my body began moving on its own. As I sailed around the living room, I performed each step of the flower routine quickly and perfectly.

Maybe Ms. Hawken had been right. All that

I needed to pull everything together was a lucky charm to boost my confidence. A sash like mine could fool even an ugly duckling into thinking she could dance like a swan.

A tired-looking Mom clapped her hands. "Lovely, dear," she said.

I gave her a hug and said, "The costume is perfect. Thanks, Mom."

But Jade had watched my dancing with a more critical eye. "You look great," she agreed. "Just be careful." She pointed to the sash hem, which reached toward the floor.

I was feeling too good for Jade's comment to annoy me now. "Don't worry," I said to my sister, my voice as full of confidence as my dance routine had been.

I couldn't *wait* for ballet class tomorrow.

CHAPTER 6

The "Lucky" Sash

Thursday morning, when Jade and I got on the bus, the aisles and seats were already filled with students carrying instruments in cases and costumes in extra bags, like us. The adult passengers looked at us as if we were all running away from home.

We created such a heavy load that I think the bus rose several inches after the dance students got off. "Hey, Isabelle!" Luisa called to me.

I hadn't even realized she'd been on the same bus. She was wearing a red bandanna tied around her head like a cap. Covering her left eye was a black eye patch.

I blinked when I saw Luisa's costume in the huge shopping bag she carried. The orange and pink flounces of her dress looked ready to explode out of the bag.

"No one's going to miss *you* onstage," I said.

She grinned at me crookedly and said, "Ha! They'd better not."

Gabriel strolled toward us from the opposite direction carrying only his backpack.

"Where's your costume?" Jade asked.

Gabriel smiled that secret smile he wears when he's doing magic tricks. He patted the stem of a flower pinned to his jacket. "You're looking at my costume," he said. "I'm going to circulate through the audience before and after the show and do a little street magic. So none of that Las Vegas flash for me."

"You're just lazy," Luisa sniffed.

Gabriel adjusted his grip on the strap of his backpack and joked, "You're just jealous."

As we joined the other students streaming into Anna Hart, I began to hum the waltz. Automatically, my arm responded, lowering like a flower petal unfolding. Jade caught the motion from the corner of her eye, and she grinned.

Once inside, we separated to head toward our lockers. Setting down the bag with my costume, I opened my locker and got to work taping my postcard of Jackie Sanchez to the inside of the locker door.

Gazing at Jackie's smiling face, I wished, "Bring me some good luck, please?" And then I closed my locker and hurried off to my first class.

Later that day, I repeated the wish when I got my costume out of the locker for the flower routine. For the next couple of days, our regular class schedule had changed. Luisa would be rehearsing with her modern dance class for the two arts periods, while I would be with my ballet class. So without

Luisa to encourage me, I knew I'd need all the luck I could get.

In the changing room, the other girls crowded around Renata, marveling at her sequined outfit. Either someone in her family was a genius at sewing, or her family had bought the outfit from a professional costumer.

No one noticed my costume right away, but I thought, *Just wait. Design is more important than a bunch of flashy sequins.* I strode confidently into the studio, feeling like a racing car with its fuel tanks full and its battery crackling with energy.

But before we began warming up, Ms. Hawken inspected our outfits. Madelyn's unitard had a pretty spray of lavender embroidered onto it. Stewart wore a headpiece cut from sheets of colored Styrofoam and assembled into a sunflower. "Good," Ms. Hawken said to him. "Your costume makes it clear just what you are."

Ms. Hawken pretended to shade her eyes when she saw the bright sequins of Renata's costume. "You're certainly going to dazzle in the spotlight," she said.

When she got to me, Ms. Hawken said, "Very pretty, Isabelle. That must have taken a lot of work." After a moment she added, "Would you turn around, please?"

As I pirouetted, my long sash twirled about me.

"Be careful of that long sash," she said before moving on to the next dancer.

I hadn't been expecting Ms. Hawken to repeat Jade's warning. After all, I was only following her advice to add some sort of lucky charm to my outfit. I forced a smile onto my face. *She'll change her mind after she sees me dance,* I told myself.

For once, I was impatient to begin performing, so our warm-ups and barre work seemed to drag on forever. Finally, though, Ms. Hawken said it was time to begin the waltz.

Now you're all going to see what I can do, I said silently to my classmates—mostly to Renata.

But as I took my place, my sash reached toward the floor like an anchor. Maybe it hadn't been such a good idea to make it so long.

Ms. Hawken started the music and sat down in a chair to watch. At home, it had been so easy to dance the waltz routine as a solo. But in class, I couldn't dance as fast or as far as I wanted because I might bump into one of the other dancers.

Every time I had to pull up to avoid bumping

into someone, my long sash brushed against my legs like a snake playing tag. It started to throw off my timing. It was making me dance worse, not better. Too late, I realized that a charm can bring *bad* luck as well as good.

How could I have been so wrong? All I wanted now was for the waltz to be over.

Then Renata whispered from behind me, "Your sash keeps getting in my way."

"Sorry," I murmured, but that distraction was enough to make me slow down. As soon as I stopped moving, the sash drooped. To my horror, the falling fabric wrapped around my legs. Suddenly I knew how a calf felt when it was lassoed and tied up at a rodeo.

All I could do was pitch forward like a chopped-down tree.

"Stop, stop," Ms. Hawken shouted before the other dancers tripped over me. The next moment, she was kneeling beside me. "Are you all right, Isabelle?"

"I'm fine," I mumbled. My cheeks felt hot. I must have been as red as an apple. Angrily I tried to stand up. When I stumbled again, my eyes filled with tears of frustration. I guess some ugly ducklings will *always* be ugly ducklings—never swans.

"You're crying," Ms. Hawken said in alarm. "Where does it hurt?"

I shook my head. *It doesn't hurt anywhere,* I wanted to say, *except inside of me.*

Angrily, I tugged at the sash—and instantly heard a loud rip. When I lifted the sash, I saw I'd ripped some of the stitching right out. I'd just wasted Mom's hard work.

"Jade was right," I mumbled as I struggled to my feet. I just wanted to get out of there.

But Renata picked up on my words. "Right about what, Dizzy Izzy?" she asked under her breath. "That you shouldn't have come here?"

"Be quiet, Renata," Ms. Hawken snapped.

But I knew that Renata was right. If I had stayed at my old school, I could have saved myself a lot of embarrassment. I was useless not only as a dancer but as a designer as well.

My classmates' faces were blurry through my watery eyes, but I thought they looked as if they were feeling sorry for me.

I couldn't take it anymore. I gathered the torn sash in my hands and rushed toward the door.

"Isabelle, where are you going?" Ms. Hawken demanded.

The "Lucky" Sash

Anywhere but here, I thought as I stumbled from the room.

I didn't get more than a few steps from the studio before I ran into my sister. "Isabelle, what's wrong?" Jade asked. In her arms, she had a stack of books from the school library.

Jade was the last person I wanted to see. She'd been right about the sash all along. I dodged around her. "Everything's wrong," I muttered, starting to run again. My torn sash streamed behind me like a banner.

"Isabelle, stop," Ms. Hawken called from the classroom door, but I kept on running.

"I'll get her, Ms. Hawken," Jade said. There was a *thump* as she set the books down on the floor.

Behind me, I heard the rapid patter of my sister's shoes.

I skidded as I turned into the corridor that led to the old building. At the end of the hall were the steps leading to the front doors.

But I never could outrun my sister. She caught me by the smiling portrait of Anna Hart, the dancer for whom the school had been named. "What happened?" Jade asked. "How did you tear your sash?"

"Let me go," I said angrily, squirming to break

free. But I'd never been able to out-wrestle my sister, either.

Jade tightened her grip. "What's going on?" she asked, leaning forward so that our foreheads were almost touching and her eyes were staring right into mine. "Tell me what's wrong."

I knew Jade wouldn't let up until I told her the truth. So I squeezed my eyes shut and took a deep breath. Then I opened my eyes and looked past Jade's concerned face—to the smiling portrait of Anna Hart—and admitted, "I just fell flat on my face in ballet class."

Jade gestured toward my waist. "I told you that sash was too long," she said matter-of-factly. "Just trim it and you'll be fine."

Jade's "I told you so" was more than I could take. I was feeling so miserable that I couldn't stop myself from saying, "The only reason I even got into this school is because of *you*. And no matter how hard I try to fit in, I don't belong here."

"Of course you do," Jade insisted.

All the hurt, all the frustration came pouring out of me now. "That's easy for you to say!" I snapped. "You're *perfect*."

Jade sucked in her breath as if I had just

punched her. "I've got my problems, too, Isabelle," she said sharply.

That only made me angrier. "Name one," I challenged her.

Jade hesitated. "None of your business," she finally said.

"Ha!" I said, jabbing an index finger at her. "You can't tell me because you don't have any problems."

Jade let go of me and slumped against a locker. "That shows what you know," she said softly. "I'm *not* perfect."

My sister suddenly looked very sad, which took the wind right out of my sails. I'd gone too far. "Sorry," I mumbled. "It's just that . . . I'm tired of everyone comparing my dancing to yours."

Jade took a deep breath. "Look," she said, "we're both good dancers. We're each better at different things."

I scoffed and shook my head. I knew better than to think I was actually better at something than Jade.

But Jade persisted. Taking a tissue from her pocket, she handed it to me. "You're better at leaps than I am, Isabelle—you really are," she said.

"Sometimes you just explode into the air. You'll be your *own* kind of dancer."

I wiped my face and looked at Jade doubtfully. "Really?"

"It's true," she said. Then she frowned thoughtfully. "You just overthink things, Isabelle. When I see you practicing at home, I can see that you're thinking about each step before you take it. You've trained your body. You have to learn to trust it."

"But how do I turn off my brain?" I wondered aloud.

Jade paused for a moment and then asked, "Have you ever tried visualization?"

Before modern dance class today, I'd never heard the word. But now I could say to Jade, "Yes, Mr. Amici just taught us about that today." I didn't mention that I had done well at it, but I began to feel more hopeful.

"Well, this is how I visualize the gypsy dance," she explained. "I imagine that I'm Tutu playing with a tassel. And I move my arms and legs the way Tutu does—up, down, and around."

It was funny to think of Jade imitating Tutu. "Is that why you spend so much time with her?" I asked.

"That's right," Jade said with a smile. "So try

it now. Imagine that you're Tutu—like this." Shutting her eyes, Jade danced a few steps effortlessly, and then opened her eyes again. "And while your mind's busy with that, your body goes through the steps on its own."

Balling up the tissue, I sighed and stepped into the middle of the hallway. As a precaution, I temporarily unwound the sash from my waist and handed it to Jade. Then I tried to picture our kitten, but unfortunately, my Tutu had started to take a nap. "It's not working," I said in frustration.

Jade chewed her lip for a moment. "Well, then, try remembering a really special time when you felt good," she suggested.

A special time? It would have to be that Saturday last summer, watching lilies in the pond in Kenilworth Park. I pictured myself floating on the pond like a water lily. Floating, circling, drifting. And I began the first steps of our dance routine.

"That's it," Jade said approvingly. "What did you imagine?"

"I was floating in a pond like a water lily," I said. And the look on Jade's face told me that I had pulled it off. Maybe there was something to this visualization thing. And that planted a small seed of hope in me. Maybe I could do this flower routine after all.

"Thanks, Jade," I said, managing a genuine smile. I couldn't be mad at her anymore—not when she was the one person who could always make me feel better. "Thanks for helping me."

"What are sisters for?" she asked, pulling me into a quick hug. Then she handed my sash back to me. "Now do something for me," she said with a smile. "Put a new hem on this."

I made a face at Jade, and she laughed as she linked arms with me. "Let's get going," she said. "Mr. Omi will be wondering what happened to those books he sent me for."

And my ballet class will be wondering what happened to me, I thought to myself, squaring my shoulders for the moment when I would have to walk back into that classroom.

When I got back to ballet, the class was in the middle of another run-through. The other students looked at me curiously but kept dancing. Only Renata smirked.

The music finished about the same time that

the school bell rang, ending the class. Before she dismissed us, Ms. Hawken reminded us that tomorrow was a big day: we would be combining our tech and dress rehearsals.

I changed back into my regular clothes, and as I was leaving for my next class, Ms. Hawken motioned for me to wait.

"Are you okay, Isabelle?" she asked kindly.

I shrugged, trying to find the words to explain what had happened. "I thought the sash on my costume would help give me confidence—like yours does," I said. "But it only made things worse."

"That's just because it was too long," she said sympathetically. "It could still work. Or you'll find your own lucky charm. It doesn't have to be anything you wear, you know. It could also be something you do."

Red-faced, I glanced toward the hallway, remembering the advice my sister had just given me. "Jade does visualization before she dances," I said, and then more softly, I added, "If it can help me dance anything like her, I'll give it a try."

Ms. Hawken smiled. "Your sister has made her share of mistakes, too, Isabelle. Anyway, you shouldn't compare yourself to her or anyone else.

Isabelle

You have to measure Isabelle against what Isabelle
can do."

But do I use inches or miles? I wondered as
I left the studio.

Jade and I didn't talk on the bus ride home. Maybe she knew I was thinking about my flower routine, wondering how I could use visualization to make it better. But she stood hip to hip with me, swaying side to side in the crowded bus aisle. That was her way of letting me know she was there if I needed more advice.

As we trudged home, I saw reminders that the Autumn Festival was coming soon. The sidewalk was hidden under a blanket of leaves. And the crisp autumn air nipped at my nose and ears. Our neighbor had raked up his leaves and put them into orange trash bags with jack-o'-lantern faces printed on them. They squatted now on his lawn like huge pumpkins. Time was rushing by too fast.

Jade unlocked the front door, and we both hurried inside. I needed to finish practicing my dance visualization, and I needed to fix my sash. But first things first. I rushed through my language arts homework at my desk.

When that was done, I took the sash from my backpack. Eagerly Tutu leaped toward it, claws reaching for the pretty dangling prey. I barely jerked it out of her way in time. "Tutu, no!" I hollered.

"I'll take her downstairs," Jade said, coming up

quickly behind me. "Tutu," she called in a high, sweet voice. From her backpack, she drew out her costume shawl and held it out like a matador's cape.

Our kitten's head twitched from side to side as the fringe of little tassels at the bottom of the shawl swung back and forth. Then, tensing, she leaped with paws outstretched to catch a tassel.

Jade jerked the shawl away at the last moment, so Tutu landed instead on the rug. Whirling around, she got ready to pounce again.

Jade jumped easily over her into the hallway and spun around, dangling the shawl once more. Tutu charged after it. The long rug in the hallway bunched up beneath her feet as she chased after Jade and disappeared from view.

I went to Mom's sewing room and started to alter the sash. Part of me thought I should wait for Mom to get home, to be sure I did the alteration right. The other part of me thought I needed to try to fix the sash myself. That part won out.

I trimmed the sash, and then I trimmed it even more, until it looked like a delicate bouquet of flowers fastened at the waist of my costume. Once I'd finished that, I stepped into my costume and tried a spin or two. Without the weight of worry over the long sash, I felt as light as a feather.

Afterward, I went to make up with Tutu. I'd just reached the foot of the stairs when I heard banging and clanking in the kitchen.

"Mom?" I called.

"Hey, Isabelle," Dad answered. "Mom phoned me. She has to work a little late, so she told me to get dinner started." He poked his head out of the kitchen. "Meatloaf okay?"

I nodded. Then I glanced down the hallway and saw Jade in the living room. She wore her shawl wrapped around her lower back and draped over her forearms. She tried a few steps as she shimmied the shawl back and forth. She was making it into a real part of her dance now. I wished I could be that creative.

When I started to feel jealous, I remembered Jade's words: "You'll be your own kind of dancer." I sighed and headed into the kitchen. I almost giggled when I saw the large oven mitts hiding Dad's hands. He looked a lot more at home behind a drum set than he did in the kitchen.

"Need any help?" I asked.

He glanced over his shoulder at me. "Peel some potatoes?" he asked hopefully. He almost tripped over Tutu, who was circling around his legs, rubbing herself against the man with the pan of meatloaf.

I got a peeler from the drawer. "Sure," I said, "since you asked so nicely."

Dad put the meatloaf into the oven. Then, as he rooted around in the drawer for another peeler, he began humming the melody of "Pond Dreams."

I shoved aside the onion that Dad hadn't used in the meatloaf. And as I started to scrape away at a potato, I hummed along in a higher pitch.

We'd peeled about three potatoes before I asked, "Dad?"

He stopped humming. "What?"

I tried to keep my voice casual as a ribbon of potato peel dropped onto the counter. "Did you ever want to become a full-time musician?" I asked.

Dad stared at the peeled potato in his hand as if it had dropped out of the sky. Then he nodded slowly. "When I was younger, I did," he said. "I had friends who became full-timers." He began to work on another potato. "But to be honest, I just wasn't as good as they were."

I thought about everything I had been feeling at Anna Hart. It was strange to find out that Dad had once felt like that, too. "Did that bother you?" I asked.

Dad swept the potato peelings into a neat pile. "For a while, it did," he admitted. "But then I realized it was useless for me to measure my talent against someone else's. And I liked the drums too much to quit. Now I just try to keep improving and to play better than I did the last time."

I patted his arm. "I think 'Pond Dreams' is your best song yet," I said, and it was true.

Dad dipped his head. "Thank you kindly," he said with a smile.

And just in case I'd never said it before, I added, "I think you're a great drummer, Dad."

"Well, maybe I've played the drums so much, I've improved a little," Dad said. "Anyway, I like to think I leave people better off after they've heard me." He wagged his peeler at me. "Now tell me why you're suddenly curious about my career decision."

Too late, I realized I shouldn't have asked so many questions—not if I wasn't prepared for Dad to start asking them, too. I picked up a carrot and began peeling it. "It's just that . . ." I began, "well, I don't think I'll ever be as good a dancer as Jade."

Dad put his peeler down and then, picking up another carrot, twirled it between his fingers. "You're going to tell this poor little carrot that's it's not as good a vegetable"—he said, reaching for a potato with his other hand—"as this tater?"

Despite everything, I started to laugh. "You're not supposed to play with your food, Dad," I scolded him.

"You're getting to sound like your mother more and more every day," said Dad. He made an elaborate show of setting both carrot and potato down side by side. "But if you're going to be fussy, you and Jade can be rubies and diamonds." Then Dad turned to face me and said, "Either way, Isabelle, stop comparing yourself to your sister." He picked up the spare onion. "That's the fastest road to onion-dom, otherwise known as the kingdom of misery and tears. Instead, just try to dance a little better than you did the day before."

At the moment, I would have settled for getting through the Autumn Festival without a mistake.

The next day in the dressing room before rehearsal, I was already nervous. Renata didn't help any when she asked, "So, how are you going to mess up today, Dizzy Izzy?"

I cringed at the nickname. When several people grinned, I wondered if I was going to be called Dizzy Izzy for the next four years. It probably all depended on the festival.

Once we were all dressed, we walked through the school corridors to the auditorium. The other classes had already started rehearsing. In the music room, about two dozen violinists played a simple tune, more or less together, as a teacher called out a tempo. Through the door of the visual arts room, I saw a teacher and four students lifting papier-mâché trees onto a wide, flat cart.

The auditorium usually served as our cafeteria, but the lunch tables had been folded up and shoved against the rear wall like giant slices of bread. The smell of the day's lunch mixed with the odor of wet paint and freshly sawn wood. Even though the door to the kitchen was shut, I could hear the clatter and clank as the staff washed dishes, big trays, and pots.

The drama students were rehearsing a scene from *The Merry Wives of Windsor* on the auditorium floor while they waited their turn onstage. Over in a corner, an *a cappella* group was practicing the song "Tomorrow." It felt like recess in here, with all the different groups playing their own games.

While our ballet class waited to go onstage, we warmed up briefly and then walked through our routine. Ms. Hawken kept time for us with claps of her hands.

After the other groups had gone on, it was finally our turn. So the other flowers and I filed past props stacked behind the stage.

Against the wall was a set that looked like a snow-covered valley. A theater arts teacher and his students were gathered there, reviewing a batch of props. Gabriel waved at me from the group.

Last night I'd worked hard on visualizing my routine. As I stepped onstage, I had just begun to run through the routine again in my mind when suddenly everything became super bright—as if I'd just been dumped onto the Sahara Desert. It was such a shock that, for a moment, I lost the dance images in my mind. Squinting, I saw Mr. Raley, the English teacher, acting as the stage manager. He began speaking into the microphone of his headset.

The light dimmed and I looked up. Overhead were banks of lights of different sizes and colors. Most of them had been turned off now.

I glanced at some of the other dancers. They

looked just as distracted as I felt. It took us a moment to find our proper places.

Ms. Hawken must have noticed. "Concentrate, class," she said from stage left.

So I tried to imagine myself back at that peaceful pond. I was tired, because I had spent most of last night running through the imagery for my dance routine. But I also was anxious to see how the shortened sash would work. I reached for it now and made a silent wish that I would finally dance well.

"Ready?" Ms. Hawken called. "Begin."

I started to move as soon as I heard the familiar music. When the notes dipped, I bent at the waist like a lily pad curling up. And when the notes rose with the harp music, I thought of the water lily opening its petals. I didn't hesitate. I knew what to do. It felt right to move my head and arms this way. All that practice was finally paying off. The good feeling made me want to move, to jump, to—!

The world suddenly went white as a spotlight swept across my eyes and moved on. Mr. Raley immediately told the student operating the spotlight to slow down.

Between the spotlight and Mr. Raley, the next image popped out of my head. When I hesitated,

Ms. Hawken made a circular gesture with her hand for me to keep going, so I did.

The spotlight, though, distracted me so much that it was hard to hold on to the images I had put together last night. The light began to follow us in time to the music, but it was moving counter-clockwise while we were wheeling in the opposite direction. I heard more barked orders, and the light started trailing us clockwise.

After about half a minute, Ms. Hawken called, "Stop, stop. Mr. Raley, it's too murky. Can you speed up making it brighter?"

"I thought you wanted twilight and then dawn," Mr. Raley said.

"My day is shorter than yours," Ms. Hawken replied. "The sun needs to come up sooner."

The music stopped, and we stood waiting while Mr. Raley and Ms. Hawken experimented with different lights until they got the combination they wanted.

Somehow we made it through our routine, but I wouldn't have called it "dancing." In fact, with all the interruptions for tech and sound adjustments, it didn't even qualify as exercise. It was more like a game of freeze tag. Our stage time ended without a complete run-through, and I didn't really get to test my modified sash.

More classes had come to the auditorium to use the stage, so we shuffled off and Ms. Hawken assembled us in a clear area of the room. "Despite all the distractions, you did well," she said, looking at me first before her eyes moved on to the rest of the class. "But you'll have a big audience tomorrow. So you'll really need to focus. Be in the studio at six."

As I left with the others to change, I wished we'd had more time onstage. I wondered if my whole class was heading toward disaster.

CHAPTER 8

Tag-Team Sewing

Late Saturday afternoon, I tried to control my growing excitement as I mounted the school steps with Jade. Inside the school, the visual arts classes had decorated the walls with pumpkins and other autumn images. Flying overhead were ghostly girls in white dresses and soldiers in blue uniforms. The old building was rumored to be haunted from the days when it had been a girls' school and later a hospital during the Civil War. I felt the ghosts' flashing red eyes watching me from the ceiling.

I could tell that some of the other students were just as keyed up as I was. They were practically skipping along the corridor, chattering away excitedly. But others were quiet, like Jade. I knew enough not to bother her while she did her visualization. As I walked with her and ran through my own set of images in my mind, I worked off some energy with arm gestures and half turns.

I glimpsed Gabriel near his locker. He was muttering to himself as he practiced a trick with his cards. Several of them slipped from between his fingers and fluttered to the floor. He scowled as he squatted and gathered up the wandering cards. His tricks might not look like magic right now, but I knew that after enough practice, they would look amazing in front of an actual audience. I hoped it would be the same with my dancing.

When we hurried by a corridor, I saw Luisa and the other pirates practicing a few steps outside the modern dance studio. They looked just as nervous as Gabriel.

We passed a woman tinkering with a video camera and tripod. Was she the videographer? I knew the school was hiring someone to record the show so that we could buy the DVD later.

Suddenly, I heard Luisa cry out in dismay. Jade and I turned at the same time to see her looking down at her costume. Even at this distance, I could see that she had torn a big hole in the side of her bodice.

"What are you going to do?" one of the pirates asked. "You can't go onstage like that."

"But I've got to," Luisa said desperately. She suddenly burst into tears.

Luisa was usually so tough. It shocked the other pirates to see her cry. I was surprised, too.

"Luisa!" I called. I motioned for her to come down to us. "It's okay. I've got a little sewing kit in my bag."

"But you have to get into your own costume,"

Luisa protested. "There's no time to fix mine."

I looked at Jade, who waved Luisa over. "There's always time to help a friend," she said. "But hurry."

As Luisa walked toward us, she started to raise an arm to wipe her face on her sleeve.

"Don't touch your face," Jade said quickly. "Your makeup will smear." We all wore makeup for performances so that our faces didn't disappear in the bright spotlight onstage.

Jade took a little packet of tissues from her bag and handed them to Luisa.

"Thanks," Luisa said, sniffling as she took a tissue.

We followed Jade to the ballet studio, and I took Luisa by the arm. "What's really wrong?" I asked her quietly. "You don't usually get this upset about things."

Luisa looked at me with wet eyes. "It's just that . . . this is the first performance my brother won't be at," she said. "We finally heard from him. He's doing okay, but he really, really wants to see my pirate dance. We're going to buy a DVD of the show to send to him. So I'm going to make sure this is one show he won't forget."

I nodded—I got that. This performance was as important for Luisa as it was for me. Maybe even more so. "You're going to be *great*," I said, squeezing her hand.

At the ballet studio, we found a handwritten sign taped to the door:

Girls only. Boys, change in the restrooms and leave your bags in Room 151.

As I opened the door, I wasn't prepared for the crowd and the confusion inside the studio. All the students from the different ballet classes were trying to get dressed at the same time. Both dressing rooms must have filled up, because girls were getting into their costumes right here in the studio. The shades had all been drawn, and ballet bags lay piled everywhere. Ms. Hawken and the other ballet teachers were discussing something intently.

"We should have left home a lot earlier," Jade said as we hunted for some clear space.

"Over here," Renata said, waving a hand from a corner of the room. "I saved a spot for you."

That startled me, until she added, "Jade, come on." She was speaking to my sister.

Isabelle

Renata was the last person I wanted to hang out with before the show. But Jade was already moving toward her, so I gripped the strap of my bag tighter and picked my way around the bags over to the corner.

Behind us, Luisa kept repeating, "Sorry, sorry." I glanced in the mirror and saw that the other ballerinas had to twist and dodge away from Luisa, or else get smothered in her outfit's fabric.

Renata had already changed into her costume. Her sequins reflected the overhead light, so there were little flashes of color every time she moved. Everything was perfect about her. Not a hair was out of place.

"Thanks," Jade said as she set her bag down beside Renata's. I sidled around them so that I could set my bag down, too.

Renata glanced at me, annoyed, when my bag bumped against her. "Sorry," I mumbled.

"I'm Renata," she said eagerly to my sister. "I don't know if you remember me?"

"Sure, you did a solo last year," Jade said politely, and then she motioned to Luisa. "But now, if you'll excuse us, we have an emergency."

"Sure, of course," Renata said, pressing herself

against the window to give us more room.

"You go on before I do, so you change first," Jade said to me. "I'll work on Luisa's costume. And then when you're done, we'll switch places."

Jade and I had to scrunch up against the mirror while Luisa got out of her costume. Then I took out my sewing kit and handed it to Jade. She sat on the bench and drew Luisa's costume onto her lap. She began threading a needle while Luisa watched anxiously over her shoulder.

I was already wearing my black unitard under my regular clothes, but I had so little room that it was hard to put on my skirt and ballet slippers. I tied the ribbons of the slippers around my ankles. Then I fastened the shortened flower sash at my waist. Since I already had on my cuff bracelet and had done my hair at home, all I needed was my tiara to complete things.

I studied my reflection in the mirror. I didn't know how my dancing would go tonight, but at least my outfit looked good.

Trying to be careful with my costume, I slowly sat down. "My turn," I said to Jade, reaching for the needle and costume.

"It's like tag-team sewing," Luisa laughed.

It was good to see her smiling again.

While my sister dressed, Renata hovered nearby. "That's a pretty costume, Jade," she piped up.

Jade wound the sash around her stomach self-consciously, hiding the narrow strip of bare skin. "Isabelle designed it," she said in response.

Renata looked at me uncomfortably. I don't think she had meant to pay me a compliment, even indirectly. "No kidding" was all she could muster. Luisa and I exchanged a secret smile.

Jade tapped me on the shoulder. "Okay, I'm done," she said. "Let me put your makeup on."

I shook my head. "No, you put yours on first," I insisted. "Let me finish this." My hand was weaving the needle back and forth in a steady rhythm. Despite the urgency, the motion was soothing and sort of hypnotic—as if my hand was dancing on its own. And as my fingertips pranced, the seam magically closed up. When I was sewing, I was never Dizzy Izzy. Maybe I felt about sewing the way Jade did about dancing.

"Ten minutes, ladies," Ms. Hawken called. "Then we all leave for the auditorium."

"Finished," I finally announced as I rose with the costume. I presented it to Luisa.

Luisa held her breath as she inspected the seam. "Isabelle, wow, you really fixed it! Thank you!" she said. She quickly stepped into the costume, and I helped her button it up. Then we stared into the mirror together as she smoothed out the bodice of the dress.

"Perfect," I said to her. "You look amazing. Danny's going to be really proud of you when he sees the DVD."

Luisa smiled—and then was silent for a long moment. "I hope so," she said finally. "Maybe he'll get homesick and call me more often."

I gave her arm a squeeze. To cheer her up, I said, "Well, the next time you're missing your older sibling, you can borrow mine. I'd gladly give her up for you."

Jade, who was applying mascara, narrowed her eyes at me in the mirror. "Hey, I heard that!" she joked.

Luisa giggled and then turned to gather her things. "Gotta go," she said. "I need to find my gang of pirates." She gave me a big thank-you and an even bigger hug, and then she turned to hug Jade, too.

As I watched Luisa force her way past the other ballerinas on her way to the door, Jade touched a fingertip to one corner of my mouth and then the other. "You know, I think this is the first time I've seen you smile at school," she said.

I shrugged. "I like sewing," I said simply. "That was fun."

"You like *helping* people," Jade said, bending over to pull a makeup brush from her kit. "Now tilt your head back. A little more. Yes, that's it. Stand still."

I watched my reflection in the mirror as she applied light beige eye shadow gently over my brow bone. That would help highlight my eyes under the bright lights. Jade's strokes were as gentle as a feather. I might be a little better at sewing than my sister, but she was a lot better at doing makeup.

While Jade put on the rest of my stage face, I had time to think about what had just happened. She was right—I felt good knowing that I'd helped Luisa, and I'd had more fun fixing her dress than I'd had in the last few rehearsals practicing to be a flower. So far, my favorite part of the festival had been creating our costumes. Maybe I should be thinking of designing rather than dancing.

Jade finished my makeup just in time. Ms. Hawken clapped her hands to get our attention.

"All right, ladies," she said. "In a few minutes, we'll leave for the auditorium. Assemble in the back with your casts. Your teacher will let you know when it's time for you to go onstage."

In the sudden pause after she finished speaking, I could hear the shuffling of a hundred feet in the corridor as the other classes headed toward the auditorium.

Jade tucked her makeup kit back into her bag. "Before a show, the kids here use part of the school motto," she said to me. She straightened with a smile. "To the stars."

"To the stars," I wished back. Then, because Renata was standing right there, I added, "To the stars, Renata."

"Yeah, ditto," Renata said.

Then the other dancers were moving toward the door, and we had no choice but to follow.

I felt my stomach getting tighter and tighter as I neared the auditorium doors.

When we got inside, I saw that chairs had been set out in even rows almost all the way back to the folded-up dining tables in the rear. Classical music played softly over the auditorium's sound system, and what looked like a hundred people—all dressed in costume—were already finding seats.

"Jade, Isabelle, over here!" Dad called. He was tall enough to see over the crowd. He kept waving as we made our way to him.

Mom was dressed tastefully in a high-waisted, Empire-style dress and carried a bone-handled fan. Dad, in contrast, had a wig that could have doubled as a mop, and it was hard to tell if the green makeup on his face was supposed to make him into a zombie or a Martian. I didn't dare ask. He would have been hurt that I hadn't recognized whatever he was pretending to be.

"Don't you two look lovely," Dad said. But he would have said that even if we had been wearing trash bags.

Mom gestured toward my flower sash. "Oh, you made it short like Jade suggested," she said.

I glanced quickly at Jade to see if she would tell

Mom about my tripping and falling. But she didn't.

And then Mom noticed something else. "Some of the flowers on your sash got squashed," she said with a sigh. Mom began pinching the cloth blossoms to fatten them up again.

She still hadn't finished when the principal, Ms. Kantor, spoke up through the sound system. "Will our guests take their seats, please? And will the casts assemble in the rear? The show will begin in ten minutes."

"Good luck," Dad murmured, giving us each a quick hug.

As I joined my ballet group at the back, Jade said good-bye to me and headed on to her gypsy band some thirty feet away. Part of me wanted to go after her. I always knew things would be okay when my big sister was with me. Without her, all my worries about the show came flooding back.

Suddenly my classmate Madelyn clutched my arm. "Oh, my gosh, that's Jackie Sanchez," she whispered loudly.

I'd seen Jackie from the second balcony of a theater, when she had looked doll-sized. But the tall woman standing in the doorway had the same olive skin and pretty smile as on the postcard in my locker.

She was wearing a red cape with a hood.

The next moment, Jackie Sanchez was joined by a chubby man with a trim blond beard and shaved head. He was wearing tails, a top hat, and a bright red scarf. I recognized him as Robert Kosloff, another graduate of Anna Hart and the director of this year's *Nutcracker*. He had conducted the auditions personally.

He was smiling, but I still felt uncomfortable around him. I remembered him as the man who kept sending away dancers at the auditions for *The Nutcracker*. Though he had tried to let dancers down in a nice way, I guess there's no way you can really be gentle about crushing someone's dreams.

Gabriel had already gone up to them and was fanning out his cards. There was nothing shy about my friend.

As Madelyn hurried past me, I asked, "Where are you going?"

"I'm going to get Jackie's autograph," she said. "Maybe she can sign my palm. I won't ever wash it again. Are you coming?"

I was tempted, but I looked at the mob of people already surging toward Jackie. It would take forever to get close to her in that crowd. And I really hadn't had time to go through my dance imagery yet. "I wish I could," I said, "but I need to get ready."

"You've already got on your costume," Madelyn said, puzzled. "But, okay—I'll see you later." She rushed away then.

Either someone had told Ms. Kantor about her special guests being mobbed, or she'd noticed it herself. The music died suddenly. Then her voice boomed over the sound system. "Will the audience please take their seats?" She phrased it politely, but anyone who attended Anna Hart would recognize the principal's tone: that was an order, not a request.

I watched as an usher in a gorilla mask escorted Jackie Sanchez and Robert Kosloff to their seats. A minute later, the auditorium went dark and conversation ended. The next moment Ms. Kantor's voice came over the speakers again. "Our first performers are Ms. Grady's first-grade ballet class, performing Rimsky-Korsakov's 'Flight of the Bumblebee.'"

The curtains drew aside, and a row of little bumblebees lined the stage. Beneath the bright lights, the first-graders got so excited that they forgot most of their dance routine. Instead, they hopped, skipped, and ran around the stage. The chaos made them seem like real bumblebees going crazy in a flower garden. They would have kept on dancing, even after their music ended, but their teacher shooed them off the stage.

The evening went by in a rush. I barely noticed the other acts. I was too busy trying to focus on that summertime pond in my mind. But it was impossible to ignore Luisa when she charged onto the stage screaming, "Dance or die!"

I didn't remember that line from rehearsals in modern dance class. The other bandanna-wearing pirates looked at one another. They didn't know what to make of Luisa either.

Maybe my friend was remembering how she'd felt when she had torn her costume and thought she couldn't go on. Or maybe she was determined to make sure that her brother would never forget this performance. I just hoped Mr. Amici didn't mind a few made-up lines.

The next moment Uncle Davi shot up from his seat. "Dance or die!" he whooped, curling his hand into a fist and pumping it into the air.

Zama rose from her seat off to the left with

Gabriel. "Dance or die!" she cried and began to clap her hands rhythmically as the techno-pop music began.

"Brava!" "Dance or die!" some of the other audience members called in response.

Encouraged by the crowd, the other pirates also roared "Dance or die!" as they poured onto the stage, moving as if they had rockets attached to their feet.

The routine was supposed to be a dance contest with a brief solo for each pirate. Of all of them, Luisa was the best. It wasn't just her colorful costume. Her positions and movements were the sharpest. And she bounced around as if she might never dance again.

She made me feel all wild and desperate and crazy inside, and I wanted to dance, too. But I was jammed at the back of the auditorium with the other performers, and there wasn't enough room. All I could do was sway back and forth. A lot of other people had caught Luisa's mood, though, because I saw their heads bobbing.

Judging by the cheers when they were done, the pirates were going to be a tough act to follow. But I wasn't worried about trying to top my friend. I just wanted to avoid being Dizzy Izzy.

When it was finally our turn to go on, I took my position with the other waltzing flowers onstage, behind the closed curtain.

I suddenly felt as if I were trapped in a small room with a cloth wall. The air was warm and still. Dust tickled my nose, and I fought the urge to sneeze. The pond now seemed as far away as the moon, and the water lily was no more than a speck in my mind. What was I going to do?

"Three," Mr. Raley counted down softly from the wings.

My heart began thumping. Jade had said I was thinking so much that I was making mistakes. It kept me from enjoying dancing. And it made me stiff and self-conscious, so I was even more likely to do something wrong.

"Two," Mr. Raley said.

Be like Luisa.

"One," Mr. Raley said.

All or nothing. Dance or die.

Gears clacked, and there were loud creaks as the curtains rolled toward either side.

I couldn't see beyond the front row, where

Jackie and the principal sat with other special guests. The lunch tables that were my landmark had vanished into the gloom, along with almost everything else. Only the faint green exit light marked where the doors were.

But even though the other rows were hidden, I could hear the audience—the rustling and crinkling of paper programs, the faint buzz of voices, the whispering of shoe soles, and the squeaking of chairs. It was as if the audience was a single living creature, not a collection of separate individuals. And all of its attention was on us.

In the darkness, waiting for the light, I suddenly remembered how the raindrops had reflected the sunlight in the park. I could see the water lily in my mind, floating on the pond. Raindrops fringed the petals' edges like jewels.

Then the French horns began calling, and the harp's rippling notes created ever-widening circles on the pond. The water lily stirred restlessly. I leaned forward, head slightly bowed, arms curved away from my sides. Then I lifted my head again as I fluttered my arms up to shoulder level.

When the spotlight came on, I almost blinked in the brilliant glare. Dust motes whirled in the

breeze that the curtains had stirred up.

In that vast darkness, I hungered for the spot-light's bright, burning circle. All on their own, my arms spread like leaves that wanted to hug the light, and my body stretched toward it. But my feet were stuck in the bottom of the pond.

As a water lily, I'd spent all my life tied to one spot on the pond. It had been frustrating because the clouds and their reflections could float where they liked, but I couldn't.

My legs lifted me like the halves of a strong, springy stem. And then suddenly I kicked free of the mud and shadowy water.

Eagerly I chased after the sun, my body loose, without any of the stiffness and awkwardness that I had felt during rehearsals. It was as if I'd taken off a tight jacket and thrown it away.

But I wasn't alone. I heard the other dancers breathing and their ballet slippers pattering over the stage. In the studio, I had always felt separate from my classmates as I tried to imitate them. But now onstage, I was one flower among many as the same breeze guided us through the familiar patterns. When they turned and spun and glided, I turned and spun and glided. And that was wonderful, too—all of us reaching together toward the sun.

As the dancers before me split into two circling rows, I thought of the flowers caught on spreading ripples of water. I bobbed my head and drifted along. With each step, I raised a leg high so that the mud wouldn't trap my feet again.

The circles unraveled into two straight lines. This was the section that had given me such trouble in class. But this time my body danced the steps perfectly. My brain felt as if it was just along for the ride.

When it was my turn to leap toward center stage, I heard Jade's voice in my head: "You just explode into the air when you leap." And I pictured a wave of water sweeping across the pond, flinging me up toward the sun. Then, for a moment, I felt as if gravity couldn't hold me anymore and I could float forever. I spread my arms wide and flew until the stage came rushing up toward me.

Renata landed at the same time I did with a soft *thump*. I could see the sweat on her shoulders and the joyful smile on her face. And then we leaped past each other to take our new places in opposite lines.

As pairs of boys and girls took turns leaping into the air, I waved my arms slowly back and forth over my head, like petals teased by a breeze. On and on we danced, changing the patterns like a living kaleidoscope.

All too soon, the music rose to a climax, but the orchestra could not hide the triangle's tinkling notes. They sparkled like tiny bubbles. Linking arms, we floated in a long line downstage—all of us now one dancer, one dance, drawing closer, ever closer toward the watching audience.

Then, just like that, it was over.

I stood there tired and panting, but happy.

This was what I wanted to do! I would gladly put up with all the hard work, worry, and trouble just as long as I could feel like this again.

And then the clapping began.

CHAPTER 10
Into the Fire

The applause was still thundering as the curtains began to close. Ms. Hawken appeared stage right and motioned for us to take the stairs as the next group came on from stage left to take our place.

I felt so happy and relieved that I had to hug somebody. I turned to the person nearest me and wrapped my arms around her. "Good job," I said to Madelyn.

"You, too," she said, patting me on the back.

Once we were in the hallway heading to the studio, I felt chilly. My costume was damp with perspiration, so I was grateful to get into the studio and dry off with a towel from my bag. I changed as quickly as I could because I wanted to see Jade dance. As I picked up my bag, though, I saw Renata moving toward the door, too.

My first impulse was to let her go first so that I wouldn't have to talk to her. But then I realized that we were going to be together for the next four years at Anna Hart—and maybe even longer if we got into Helen Tischler, the performing arts high school.

So I forced myself to catch up with her and smile politely. "Good job back there, Renata," I said with as much sincerity as I could muster.

She drew her eyebrows together and gave me a

suspicious look as if to ask, *Why are you being nice
to me?*

"And thanks for saving a spot for us to dress,"
I added. "I appreciate it."

I think Renata was more comfortable fighting with me than being friendly. But she gave a little
grunt. "You didn't embarrass yourself tonight," she
said. "Congrats."

"Uh . . . thanks," I said.

The rest of our classmates had already left
the studio, but I could hear them talking happily
outside in the hallway. Ms. Hawken was standing by
the doorway with her ring of keys. She winked in
approval when she saw me walking with Renata.

When we finally left, Ms. Hawken turned off
the lights and locked the door again. Then the three
of us headed back toward the auditorium.

We got there just in time for Jade. I crossed my
fingers as I heard the music from *Carmen* begin—even
though I knew my sister didn't really need any luck.

Dressed as gypsies, Jade's ballet class strutted
onstage with arched feet. But only Jade's feet were
curved perfectly. Even though I had seen her practice
this routine at home, that had been like seeing the
sketch of a costume. Now I was seeing the real thing.

The shawl hung across her lower back. Curious as a kitten, Jade raised one corner so that she could bat the tiny tassels Mom had sewn along the hem. Playing with the shawl, she danced across the stage. I felt a lump form in my throat as she twisted and arched with the easy grace of a cat. Every movement of her arms and legs, every pose, was lovely and exact.

It was like watching Tutu dance on two legs. No, it was like watching a Tutu who weighed next to nothing. Every kick of Jade's legs and every sweep of her arms made it seem as if she were hovering over the boards.

Jade's gypsies got the loudest applause of the evening, even louder than the pirates. Renata and I did our part, clapping loudly and excitedly. When the curtains finally closed on my sister, my palms tingled.

"Jade was beautiful," Renata murmured admiringly.

So we agreed on something after all.

Renata hefted her bag to her shoulder. "One of these days, I'm going to be even better than your sister, you know," she declared.

I doubted that, but I didn't say anything. No one was as good as Jade—not Renata and certainly

not me. But tonight, I was okay with that. I had
danced well—really well—and I was glad that Jade
had, too.

Renata started to walk toward the doors, but
after a few steps, she glanced at me over her shoulder
and said, "See you Monday."

I guess that was her way of admitting that
I belonged at Anna Hart after all.

I grinned and said, "Yeah, Monday."

As soon as my family got home, I dropped my
bag in the hallway. "Dibs on the shower," I said, beat-
ing Jade to it.

"Go ahead," Jade said. "I've got plenty of time.
I'm too excited to be able to sleep anytime soon."

I knew what she meant. I was tired, but I could
feel the adrenaline still rushing through me, too.

Tutu strutted toward us down the hallway,
waving the tip of her tail high in the air like a flag.
She seemed annoyed when Mom didn't immediately
provide treats or petting.

Instead, Mom reached into her pocket for her
phone. "It's an e-mail from the HDC," she said, check-
ing the screen. "Oh—cast lists for *The Nutcracker*!"

"Let's see!" said Jade, reaching for the phone. Mom gave it to Jade and then stood to the side, her hand covering her mouth. I know she was just as excited—and nervous—about this as we were.

"Hurry up! Read it," I said, looking over Jade's shoulder.

Jade was already scrolling through the e-mail. When I didn't see Jade's name right away, I thought my sister had been robbed. We kept reading, though.

When I saw Jade's name in the third cast, I let out a scream that sent Tutu skittering away from us.

"You're going to be Clara. You got a lead role!" I shouted, grabbing Jade's arm and hopping up and down.

Poor Jade. I was yanking her around so much that she almost dropped the phone. But somehow she managed to keep scrolling down.

Jade let out a shriek the next moment. "Isabelle, you're in the cast, too!" she said excitedly.

"Huh, I am?" I said, stunned. Jade held out her phone for me to see. There it was in black and white: *Isabelle Palmer*. I was going to be one of Mother Ginger's children. "I am! I am!" I squealed. And then I saw Luisa's name, too. This was more than I had hoped for. There had been so many talented dancers at the audition, and yet we'd somehow managed to get roles.

Letting go of Jade, I began bouncing around the hallway as our parents grinned. I hadn't thought I could ever feel this happy.

I stopped only when my sister wrapped her arms around me and held me tight. "It's always been my dream to be in *The Nutcracker* with you, Isabelle," she said. "And now we are!"

"We're so proud of you," Dad said, wrapping us up in a bear hug. Mom joined us with a hug from behind.

"See?" she said, reaching out to tousle my hair. "I knew you'd both be in *The Nutcracker.*"

But then fear replaced happiness as a new thought hit me. *I barely made it through a school festival in an auditorium. How am I going to handle a professional production in a real, honest-to-goodness theater?*

My stomach dropped. Talk about jumping from the frying pan into the fire.

Letter from American Girl

Dear Readers,

Isabelle attends a special school that celebrates the performing arts. Here are the stories of four real girls who practice the performing arts, too.

Read about Reagan, who attends a full-time ballet academy; Marlo and Joia, who perform circus arts, such as clowning and trapeze; and Emily, who composes her own music. All of these girls have something in common: like Isabelle, they have followed their passions and discovered their own ways to shine.

As you read these stories, think about the ways in which you let your best self shine, too.

Your friends at American Girl

A Passion for Dance

Reagan W.
Age 12

I go to a full-time ballet academy. I love to dance! We practice hard in the studio—about four hours a day. We also go to class, do homework, eat, and study, study, study. We always find time for fun, too, like playing basketball and eating ice cream.

Last year was my first year at the ballet academy. For our spring performance, I danced a solo *en pointe*, which means that I danced on my toes. The solo was a little scary, but I was so happy to have earned such a privilege. I wore a sparkly blue-and-gold tutu and lots

The sparkly blue-and-gold tutu I wore for the performance

Going to class wtih friends Hannah and Meiri

of makeup, including bright pink lipstick. The tutu looked light and pretty, but it was very heavy. The dress fitter made sure that it fit me perfectly.

Living at school is a lot different from living at home. My room at school has a sink, a few drawers, a closet, and a bunk bed. I live on the third floor with all of the younger kids. Sometimes I get homesick

Vocabulary

• grand battement (grahn baht-mahn): a ballet movement in which you lift one leg up in the air and then bring it down

• tendu (tahn-doo): a ballet movement in which you slide one foot along the floor until it's pointed

• en pointe (ahn pwahnt): dancing on your toes in special ballet slippers called pointe shoes

for my family back in Texas, and I had to learn how to do my own laundry. But I call home a couple of times a day, and I call my grandma once a week. I hope that all my hard work will help me get into a good ballet company when I'm done with school. Maybe I'll even be a famous ballerina someday.

I always try to make sure that my form is just right.

Remember to pack in my dance bag:

- Extra ballet slippers

- Elastic bands or straps to help me stretch

- A dance video to watch and practice

A quiet moment in the studio

A Double Act

What's more fun than going to the circus? Being in the circus! But it's hard work, too. Read on to learn more about these two sisters, who study and perform the circus arts—together.

Sisters Joia G., age 9, and Marlo G., age 10

Marlo G.'s Balancing Act

Yep, when you're first learning to walk a tightrope, you fall off—a lot. (It's a good thing that the wire I walk is low to the ground!) But with really good balance and a lot of practice, it's possible to learn to walk carefully but confidently across a narrow metal strand—and to make it to the other side safely.

There are lots of different circus arts. My sister, Joia, does clowning and has tried other acts, and I've trained in several of them, too. Besides low wire (the name for the low tightrope that I use), I also do triple trapeze. That's a large trapeze separated into three different parts, one for each performer. Three of us work as a team to perform complex tricks. On triple trap, it's all about teamwork and trust—you have to be confident that your team won't let you fall. And once you've worked together for a while, you know that they won't.

Staaay steady . . .

Just hanging around!

Joia G., Clowning Around

At the circus, sometimes more than one act is going on at once. When that happens, I work hard to get the audience's attention and to wow them with what I can do. Onstage, I have to stay focused and confident—and to smile so hard that my cheeks cramp. But that's not hard to do when I'm having so much fun.

Rehearsing my act

I'm a clown. If you're in the audience when I'm performing at the circus, it's my goal to get you laughing. If you are frowning or looking at me strangely and not laughing at all, here are some things I might try:

• Doing a weird dance
• Telling you a joke
• Talking to you in an odd accent
• Sitting next to you and stealing popcorn
• Singing—laaaa!

Really, though, clowning is serious business (well, kind of). The other clowns and I take classes and train our bodies and brains to react to situations in funny ways. I know how to fall flat on the ground and make the audience think I really fell, which is pretty funny. I've learned to keep myself from laughing when everyone else is laughing (even though I still cross my fingers and hope that I don't crack up, too!).

I feel proud when I have people in stitches. If everyone's laughing, I'm happy—it means that I've done my job well.

"Breathing" Music

I started taking piano lessons right before I turned five, but it feels as if I've been playing my whole life. When I sit at a piano, music flows out of me, just like breath.

Emily B.
Age 9

Learning the music of other composers is important, but I also write my own pieces. I find music everywhere. I've written songs about things I see in nature, people I meet, and stuff I read in books. My family likes playing a game in which they shout out something—such as "raindrops sliding down a window!"—and hearing what song I can make to match it.

Playing the piano is easy for me, but I still work hard at it. I usually practice for a few hours a day, and formal lessons take up a few hours a week. When I'm getting ready for a big performance, I practice more often. I've gotten to do some fun performances at music festivals, in major concert halls, at the White House, in other countries, and even on TV.

Mostly I don't feel different from anyone else. I like baking and making crafts and playing outside. But it's so exciting when I get letters from people I don't know—sometimes from halfway around the world. People write letters saying that they like my music, or that they've learned to play some of my pieces from my published music books or else from videos they have found online. It doesn't make me feel famous, though—that's not what matters to me. I just like to know that people feel happy when they hear my music. That makes me feel really good.

Performing at the White House

About the Author

Laurence Yep is the author of more than 60 books. His numerous awards include two Newbery Honors and the Laura Ingalls Wilder medal for his contribution to children's literature. Several of his plays have been produced in New York, Washington, D.C., and California.

Though *The Nutcracker* was a regular holiday treat for Laurence as a boy, it was his wife, Joanne Ryder, who really showed him how captivating and inspiring dance can be with her gift of tickets to the San Francisco Ballet. Their seats were high in the balcony, yet they were able to see the graceful, expressive movements of the dancers far below.

Laurence Yep's books about Isabelle are his latest ones about ballet and a girl's yearning to develop her talents and become the dancer she so wishes to be.